Pr

and his Pas.

"Keating has accumulated an impressive assortment of characters in his series, and he gives each of them ample opportunity to shine... As in the preceding novels, the author skillfully blends Grant's sermonizing with intermittent bouts of violence. It creates a rousing moral quandary for readers to ponder without either side overwhelming the storyline. Tight action scenes complement the suspense (uncertainty over when the next possible attack will be) ... The villains, meanwhile, are just as rich and engrossing as the good guys and gals. The familiar protagonist, along with sensational new and recurring characters, drives an energetic political tale."

- *Kirkus Reviews* on *Reagan Country*

"In this short story, Keating's recurring cleric Stephen Grant steps up to help a popular comic-book creator targeted by armed assailants... When kidnappers eventually abduct someone, Stephen is quickly on their trail, and he has plenty of help – a convention's worth of superheroes. The series' protagonist remains a man of action even though the story isn't novel-length. This relatively short piece is lighter in tone than previous outings, due mainly to its concentration on the cheery setting. Keating respectfully portrays the con as a mostly enjoyable experience... An entertaining, immersive jaunt with a formidable protagonist."

- *Kirkus Reviews* on *Heroes and Villains*

"It was my great privilege that Ronald Reagan and I were good friends and political allies. This exciting political thriller may be a novel but it truly captures President Reagan's optimism and principles."

- Ambassador Fred J. Eckert on *Reagan Country*

"First-rate supporting characters complement the sprightly pastor, who remains impeccable in this thriller."

- Kirkus Reviews on *Lionhearts*

"A first-rate mystery makes this a series standout..."

- Kirkus Reviews on *Wine Into Water*

"Ray Keating has created a fascinating and unique character in Pastor Grant. The way Keating intertwines politics, national security and faith into a compelling thriller is sheer delight."

- Larry Kudlow
formerly CNBC's *The Kudlow Report* and
current director of the National Economic Council

"The author packs a lot into this frantically paced novel... a raft of action sequences and baseball games are thrown into the mix. The multiple villains and twists raise the stakes... Stephen remains an engaging and multifaceted character: he may still use, when necessary, the violence associated with his former professions, but he at least acknowledges his shortcomings – and prays about it. Action fans will find plenty to love here, from gunfights and murder sprees to moral dilemmas."

- Kirkus Reviews on *Murderer's Row*

Murderer's Row was named KFUO's BookTalk "Book of the Year" in 2015.

The River was a 2014 finalist for KFUO's BookTalk "Book of the Year."

"Ray Keating is a great novelist."

"A gritty, action-stuffed, well-considered thriller with a gun-toting clergyman."

"President Ronald Reagan's legacy will live on in the U.S., around the world and in the pages of history. And now, thanks to Ray Keating's *Reagan Country*, it will live on in the world of fiction. *Reagan Country* ranks as a page-turning thriller that pays homage to the greatest president of the twentieth century."

"Mr. Keating's storytelling is so lifelike that I almost thought I had worked with him when I was at Langley. Like the fictitious pastor, I actually spent 20 years working for the U.S. intelligence community, and once I started reading *The River*, I had to keep reading because it was so well-crafted and easy to follow and because it depicted a personal struggle that I knew all too well. I simply could not put it down."

"Must read for any Reaganite."

"Thriller and mystery writers have concocted all manner of main characters, from fly fishing lawyers to orchid aficionados and former ballplayers, but none has come up with anyone like Stephen Grant, the former Navy Seal and CIA assassin, and current Lutheran pastor. Grant mixes battling America's enemies and sparring with enemies of traditional Christian values, while ministering to his Long Island flock. The amazing thing is that the character works. The Stephen Grant novels are great reads beginning with *Warrior Monk*, which aptly describes Ray Keating's engaging hero."

- David Keene, former American Conservative Union chairman, former National Rifle Association president, and former opinion editor at *The Washington Times*

"*Warrior Monk* by Ray Keating has all of the adventure, intrigue, and believable improbability of mainstream political thrillers, but with a lead character, Pastor Stephen Grant, that resists temptation."

- *Lutheran Book Review* on *Warrior Monk*

Marvin Olasky, editor-in-chief of WORLD magazine, lists Ray Keating among his top 10 Christian novelists.

Shifting

Sands

A Pastor Stephen Grant Short Story

Ray Keating

All the best!

Ray Keating

For more information:
Keating Reports, LLC
P.O. Box 596
Manorville, NY 11949
raykeating@keatingreports.com

ISBN-13: 9781730956867

Cover design by Tyrel Bramwell.

*For
Jonathan,
David
and
Beth*

Previous Books by Ray Keating

Heroes & Villains: A Pastor Stephen Grant Short Story
(2018)

Reagan Country: A Pastor Stephen Grant Novel (2018)

Lionhearts: A Pastor Stephen Grant Novel (2017)

Wine Into Water: A Pastor Stephen Grant Novel (2016)

Murderer's Row: A Pastor Stephen Grant Novel (2015)

The River: A Pastor Stephen Grant Novel (2014)

An Advent for Religious Liberty:
A Pastor Stephen Grant Novel (2012)

Root of All Evil? A Pastor Stephen Grant Novel (2012)

Warrior Monk: A Pastor Stephen Grant Novel (2010)

In the nonfiction arena...

The Realistic Optimist TO DO List & Calendar 2019 (2018)

Unleashing Small Business Through IP:
The Role of Intellectual Property in Driving
Entrepreneurship, Innovation and Investment
(Revised and Updated Edition, 2016)

Unleashing Small Business Through IP:
Protecting Intellectual Property, Driving Entrepreneurship
(2013)

Discussion Guide for Warrior Monk:
A Pastor Stephen Grant Novel (2011)

"Chuck" vs. the Business World: Business Tips on TV
(2011)

U.S. by the Numbers:
What's Left, Right, and Wrong with America State by State
(2000)

New York by the Numbers:
State and City in Perpetual Crisis (1997)

D.C. by the Numbers: A State of Failure (1995)

"Everyone then who hears these words of mine and does them will be like a wise man who built his house on the rock. And the rain fell, and the floods came, and the winds blew and beat on that house, but it did not fall, because it had been founded on the rock. And everyone who hears these words of mine and does not do them will be like a foolish man who built his house on the sand. And the rain fell, and the floods came, and the winds blew and beat against that house, and it fell, and great was the fall of it."

- Matthew 7:24-27

"On Christ, the solid Rock, I stand; All other ground is sinking sand."

- Edward Mote
"My Hope is Built on Nothing Less"

"It's hard to give a career like this up, when I tell my wife I'm going to the office, and it's the beach."

- Karch Kiraly
Beach volleyball legend

Brief Dossiers on Recurring Characters

Pastor Stephen Grant. After college, Grant was a Navy SEAL and then worked at the CIA. He subsequently became a Lutheran pastor, serving at St. Mary's Lutheran Church on the eastern end of Long Island. Grant grew up in Ohio, just outside of Cincinnati. He possesses a deep knowledge of theology, history, and weapons. His other interests include archery, golf, writing, movies, the beach, poker and baseball, while also knowing his wines, champagnes and brews. Stephen Grant is married to Jennifer Grant.

Jennifer Grant. Jennifer is a respected, sought-after economist. Along with Yvonne Hudson and Joe McPhee, she is a partner in a consulting firm. Her first marriage to then-Congressman Ted Brees ended when the congressman had an affair with his chief of staff. Jennifer loves baseball (a Cardinals fan while her husband, Stephen, cheers on the Reds) and literature, and has an extensive sword and dagger collection. Jennifer grew up in the Las Vegas area, with her father being a casino owner.

Father Tom Stone. A priest and rector at St. Bartholomew's Anglican Church on Long Island, Tom is one of Grant's closest friends, and served as Stephen's best man. He enjoyed surfing while growing up in southern California, and is known for an easygoing manner and robust sense of humor. Along with Stephen, Tom and two other friends regularly meet for morning devotions and conversation at a local diner, and often play golf together. Tom is married to Maggie Stone, who runs her own public relations business. They are the parents to six children.

Paige Caldwell. For part of Stephen Grant's time at the CIA, Paige Caldwell was his partner in the field and in the bedroom. After Stephen left the Agency, Paige continued with the CIA until she eventually was forced out. However, she went on to start her own firm, CDM International

Strategies and Security, with two partners – Charlie Driessen and Sean McEnany.

Charlie Driessen. Charlie was a longtime CIA veteran, who had worked with both Stephen Grant and Paige Caldwell. Driessen left the Agency to work with Paige at CDM. Prior to the CIA, he spent a short time with the Pittsburgh police department.

Phil Lucena. Charlie Driessen brought Phil from the CIA to work at CDM. Lucena is well known for his courteousness, as well as expertise in close combat.

Jessica West. Paige Caldwell wooed Jessica away from the FBI to join CDM. West thinks fast and acts accordingly. She has suffered major losses, with her father and brother, both Marines, dying in Afghanistan and Iraq, respectively, and her fiancé, a fellow FBI agent, perishing in a terrorist attack in New York City. She came to work at CDM in part to dispense a kind of harsh justice that would not have been possible with the FBI.

Sean McEnany. After leaving the Army Rangers, Sean McEnany joined the security firm CorpSecQuest, which was part legitimate business and part CIA front. He later signed up with Caldwell and Driessen at CDM. He maintains close contact with the CIA; and has a secret, high-security office in the basement of his suburban Long Island home, along with a mobile unit disguised as a rather typical van parked in the driveway. McEnany's ability to obtain information across the globe has an almost mystical reputation in national security circles. For good measure, Sean, his wife, Rachel, and their children attend St. Mary's Lutheran Church, where Stephen Grant is pastor.

Chase Axelrod. Chase worked with Sean McEnany at CorpSecQuest, and then became an employee of CDM. He grew up in Detroit, became a star tight end with a 4.0 grade point average in college, and then earned a master's degree in foreign languages from N.C. State. He has mastered six foreign languages – Mandarin, German, French, Russian, Spanish and Japanese.

Chapter 1

Melissa Ambler took a stride forward, and tossed the white, blue and yellow ball high against the azure sky. She jumped in the air, and slapped a serve that skimmed just above the net. The ball hit the sand between the two frozen opponents, and just inside the end line. Ambler and her partner, Ranya Khan, pumped their fists, exchanged a high five, and urged each other forward.

Meanwhile, thumping, high energy music played on unrelentingly. The beat even continued during the action, though at lower decibels than between points. There was no indication that the players cared or were distracted, and the fans loved it.

Like many spots up and down the California coastline, the sands of Manhattan Beach ranked as familiar terrain for beach volleyball. Of course, this particular event was far beyond a local pick-up match or amateur league. This was professional beach volleyball, with men's and women's two-person teams competing for not-so-insignificant purses. And they played before a few thousand fans packed into a temporary stadium erected between the waves of the Pacific Ocean to the west, and palm trees and the city of Manhattan Beach to the east, while sitting alongside the famous pier.

Manhattan Beach had served as a stop for the pros since the 1980s, and the 928-foot Manhattan Beach Pier included plaques of the "Volleyball Walk of Fame."

This new tour called itself "Bedlam on the Beach."

*   *   *

Three men stood together at the intersection of Manhattan Avenue and Manhattan Beach Blvd. Waiting to cross the street, they shifted slightly from side to side, with their eyes looking down at the sidewalk and then up, darting around. The light changed, and they resumed their westward trek.

The sidewalk gently declined toward the Manhattan Beach Pier, and compared to the others strolling in that direction, the three appeared out of place. Contrary to the casual, generally beach-friendly attire worn by most on this warm and sunny day, the three men sported long coats. That drew some brief glances, but nothing more. After all, this was California, and out-of-the-ordinary wasn't all that out of the ordinary.

*   *   *

What exactly allowed the Bedlam on the Beach Tour to claim the label 'bedlam"? It ramped up the excitement by placing two regulation-sized beach volleyball courts next to each other in the main stadium, with two matches going on at the same time. This wasn't how big-time beach volleyball was done – until now.

Bedlam on the Beach offered a flurry of serves, spikes, digs, blocks, aces and rallies side by side, with the crowd shouting at and cheering for what was going on in two matches. Eyes jumped back and forth between the contests, with fans sometimes not sure where to look. The players on one court had to stay focused no matter what might be occurring next to them or how the crowd might be reacting. It did, in fact, have non-stop energy and a bedlam-like quality. Again, fans loved it.

At this moment on a Sunday afternoon in late May, the men's final was being played right next to the women's. Each match had moved into a third, decisive set. On the women's court – which only varied from the men's by having a slightly lower height for the net – Melissa Ambler and Ranya Khan were trying to upset the heavily favored team of Kelsey Gale and Sunny Sackett.

Ambler, with her long blond hair pulled back in a ponytail, offered another quality serve, but this time Gale responded with an impressive dig. Sackett then provided a near-perfect set as Gale returned to her feet. On one side of the net, Gale, in a dark blue bikini, jumped into the air, with the tall Ambler, sporting her team's bright yellow bikini, doing the same on the other side. Gale went for the spike, and Ambler for the block. Ambler's quick thinking, height and formidable leaping ability went a long way in making up for her team's relative inexperience. At first, it appeared that Ambler's block was successful, but after the ball ricocheted off her right hand, it hit the sand a few inches out of bounds.

*   *   *

The beach volleyball courts and stands were positioned so that some non-paying fans walking on the Manhattan Beach Pier could catch glimpses of the action. Among those able to see the courts from the pier, two chose instead to watch the individuals milling about on the pier. Likewise, two others inside the stadium had eyes trained on the crowd in the stands rather than on the players.

CDM International Strategies and Security had been hired to provide extra security for Bedlam on the Beach – specifically for one of the players. Paige Caldwell, one of CDM's owners, and three of the firm's employees were on hand. Caldwell and Phil Lucena, both former CIA, were on the pier, while Jessica West, onetime FBI, and Brooke Semmler, who previously had been with the Secret Service, were on watch in the stadium. West and Semmler actually had entered the tournament as a team, and after being eliminated on Thursday, the first day of competition, they were able to move freely throughout the remaining days of the event.

Lucena spotted the three men in long coats approaching the pier. He then made eye contact with Caldwell. All four CDM personnel wore small microphones and tiny earpieces that few people on the planet would be able to detect. Caldwell whispered, "Pictures to Sean."

Lucena responded, "Right."

Phil Lucena possessed deadly skills, particularly in close combat. Not many would gather this from his appearance or demeanor, in particular an easy smile, brown hair and a thin beard, a stocky five-foot-six-inch frame, and a penchant for extreme politeness. He currently played the role of tourist, donning a Route 66 t-shirt, cargo shorts, and white sneakers. Lucena turned his smartphone, zoomed in with the camera, and snapped pictures of each man.

Lucena quickly sent the photos to Sean McEnany, who was seated in his secure office on the other coast in the basement of his suburban Long Island home. Lucena's text read, "Need IDs ASAP, please." He then whispered, "Sent to Sean."

"Thanks," replied Caldwell. "Let's keep these three as close as possible."

*   *   *

The crowd erupted as a spike ended the men's final.

Before she served, Sunny Sackett paused to let the victors on the neighboring court savor the win. As the announcer declared the final score and names of the winners, the two men's teams shook hands with each other, the referees and line judges. The victors proceeded to wave at the cheering crowd. That celebration would resume after the women's final was finished.

The music was kicked up, once again. Sackett took a deep breath, and sent her serve over the net.

Other than some sets of eyes looking at their phones, Jessica West and Brooke Semmler were the only people in the stands not paying attention to the action on the sand.

Khan handled the serve, and an extended rally ensued, filled with spikes, digs and blocks – all appreciated by the crowd – until Gale lofted a soft shot over both Khan and Ambler, who were out of position after managing to return a spike by Sackett. The ball landed in a back corner of the court. Gale and Sackett would now serve match point.

* * *

The three men in long coats quickened their pace after stepping onto the pier. They glanced at each other, and then moved along the north side of the pier, which was largely clear as people were focused on looking off the south side at the volleyball courts.

Caldwell said, "I don't like this. We can't wait for Sean. Move now, Phil."

He replied, "Moving."

* * *

Ambler once again jumped into the air trying to block a spike from Gale. But while the ball glanced against her left hand, its trajectory was only slightly altered. Khan dove, and with a fist, actually kept the point alive. The ball flew forward, hit the net, and started to fall back toward the sand floor. But Ambler extended her body, and managed to pop the volleyball high into the air.

The ball reached its apex, and began its return to earth.

Sackett's wide eyes were hidden by sport sunglasses. As her tanned body rose to meet the descending sphere, her habit of pushing the tip of her tongue out on a kill shot took over.

Ambler and Khan managed to jump to their feet, but they were moving backward, on the defensive.

Sackett grunted as her right hand crashed against the volleyball, sending it on a descending, accelerating path. To the amazement of all in the stadium, including Sunny

Sackett, Melissa Ambler managed to lunge and get a hand on the ball before it hit the sand.

The crowd reacted in unison to Ambler's feat.

But it was to no avail. The ball flew in the wrong direction, going sideways in the direction of the stands.

*   *   *

While the crowd on the pier pressed forward to see match point play out, Lucena moved quickly in the opposite direction. He approached the three men from behind.

Caldwell broke out of the crowd, coming face to face with the first of the three men in coats. While she was moving quickly, the man initially had little reason to be concerned. After all, Caldwell was dressed like so many others, sporting a white, strapless top under a red cotton linen roll sleeve shirt, light blue jeans, a headband pulling back her long black hair, and dark sunglasses.

But as she approached, the man froze in front of Caldwell. His coat swung open for the first time, revealing an Uzi SMG.

As Caldwell sprang forward, she announced to her CDM colleagues, "Gun." Before the terrorist could respond, Paige Caldwell struck. Her fist plunged into the man's neck, crushing the trachea. As he instinctively reached for his throat, Caldwell continued her movement forward, lowering herself slightly, and then pushing up. She sent the man over the side of the pier. The shallow waves did not help him. When his head hit the sand, the snapping of his neck spared him the helplessness of dying via suffocation.

*   *   *

Upon hearing Caldwell's call of "Gun," Lucena removed a tactical knife that had been nestled next to a Glock under the Route 66 shirt.

He broke into a sprint. Moving to the left of the third long-coated figure, Lucena backhanded the knife, and then drove into the man's neck. The shocked terrorist struggled to suck in air. Lucena pulled the knife out. As the man fell to his knees, Lucena shifted his attention to the final threat. That terrorist started to reach for his Uzi.

Lucena led with the knife. He shoved it into the assailant's stomach, while wrapping his left arm around the man's back. Nonetheless, the terrorist still managed to pull the Uzi free. With the gun out, Lucena let go of the knife, leaving it protruding from his opponent's stomach, and grabbed hold of the big coat. Lucena turned both their bodies, and pushed himself up onto the pier's railing.

Nearby, people started to focus on the altercation.

Lucena rolled his back over the railing, pulling the terrorist onto himself, and then the two disappeared over the side.

*　*　*

The crowd cheered as the ball was batted by two fans in the stands before one was able to secure it. Sackett and Gale threw their arms into the sky, and then hugged each other.

On her knees, Khan simply stared at the victors, while Ambler was lying face down in the sand.

Khan rose to her feet first, came over, and helped Ambler up. As they hugged, Khan said, "I thought we had them."

Ambler nodded, and replied, "Me, too."

They turned and shook hands with the victors.

*　*　*

With her Glock now in hand, Caldwell glanced at the only terrorist who was still on the pier. He was lying face down, with blood flowing from the deep, fatal knife wound in his neck. She looked back over the railing down at three unmoving bodies. The two attackers were face down, with Lucena on his back. The waters of the Pacific sloshed around and over each body, with trails of blood mixing with the salt water.

As Caldwell moved toward the body of the terrorist lying on the pier, she waved at three approaching local police officers, urging them to move more quickly. She whispered a brief explanation to one of the officers, who got on his radio. Caldwell then slipped her gun back into the holster in the small of her back and started sprinting down the pier. Additional officers on the beach moved in on the bodies lying on the beach. Caldwell found a spot where she could safely launch herself over the pier's railing. She landed softly in a crouch, steadied herself with a left hand in the sand, and then ran toward Phil Lucena.

Chapter 2

Three months later...

Stephen Grant had mastered an assortment of skills as a Navy SEAL. Later, his repertoire of abilities was both fine-tuned and expanded while at the Central Intelligence Agency. And then came four years of very different training at the seminary, and his subsequent extended period of time as a parish pastor.

But his prowess over a wide breadth of abilities – from profiling to prayer – mattered little right now. There was no way out. Traffic on the Long Island Expressway crept ever so slowly toward the Midtown Tunnel, leaving Grant no alternatives or escape routes for his Mojave Sand-colored, four-door Jeep Wrangler. But it really didn't matter. Grant was in no hurry. He enjoyed the company.

His wife, Jennifer Grant, sat next to him on the passenger side, and in the backseat was Father Tom Stone, one of his closest friends.

Grant was largely in listening mode while Jennifer and Tom discussed a mutual friend, Melissa Ambler.

Jennifer said, "Yes, I'm worried about her, too. We haven't talked much recently. She's so busy."

Tom nodded. "Ever since Mike died, she's moved deeper and deeper into her work."

Been there. Grant observed, "Busy isn't necessarily bad, and it's not unusual. It's a pretty typical coping mechanism."

"I get it," replied Tom. "But it's been a few years now, and she seems to be doing the work thing to the exclusion of everything else. She's running Corevana as well as the education foundation; started up and is playing in this Bedlam on the Beach Professional Volleyball Tour; and has returned to modeling. Each of those could be a fulltime gig. The only thing she's stepped back from is the baseball team. And even there, from what I've heard, she keeps pretty close tabs on Ty Beachamp."

Stephen reflected, "I forgot that she hired Ty to run things as team president."

Corevana Entertainment, a video gaming company, had made Mike Vanacore a billionaire by the time he was 26. When Mel and Mike started dating, given his business status and her international modeling fame, they earned near-global attention, from *Forbes* to the SI swimsuit issue, from Fashion Avenue to Silicon Valley. Significant swathes of the media, tech community and fashion business, however, could never really figure out what to do with the couple's faith. The awkwardness of an interviewer was unmistakable when, for example, Melissa replied to a question about the couple being at an event in defense of religious liberty. Melissa had said, "Our Christian beliefs are central to both of us. They helped create the people we are today."

While on Long Island, at their home in Quogue, Mike and Melissa were members and attended St. Bartholomew's Anglican Church, where Tom was the rector. Tom performed their marriage ceremony, and was counted as a friend.

But then Mike was murdered.

Stephen inched forward in traffic. He said, "I was glad to see that the league continued, although I do miss being one of the Surf Kings' chaplains." For the team's first season, Mike and Melissa asked Tom to be the team chaplain. Given time constraints, he turned it into a squad of four handling the chaplain duties. Tom drafted Stephen, along with their

Shifting Sands   11

two friends, Pastor Zackary Charmichael and Father Ron McDermott.

Tom replied, "The chaplaincy was one of the few things that Melissa let go. And then after about a year, she started coming to church less and less when at the Quogue house, and I don't think she's attending at all while in California." He paused. "I've been increasingly worried that she's drifting away."

Jen said, "Me, too."

Tom continued, "That's one of the reasons why I was so pleased that Melissa decided to hire Maggie to do the PR work for the volleyball tour." He added, "Maggie and I are going to have dinner with her tonight."

Jen said, "I hope it goes well."

Tom nodded. "I pray we can at least talk and find out what's going on."

After a minute of silence, Stephen shifted gears. "Please thank Maggie again for inviting Jen and me. This will be my first time at a beach volleyball event, and we're sitting courtside to boot."

Tom responded, "I'll pass it along, although you'll obviously see her running around the event. And you're going to love the competition. It's great. Beach volleyball was part of my younger days."

"Well, you were a Southern California guy," observed Stephen. "Surfing, volleyball on the beach, and what else?"

Tom smiled. "Cars and pretty girls."

Jennifer gave a slight roll of the eyes, and interjected, "I get the feeling you guys are going to start singing a Beach Boys tune."

"I like your thinking." Stephen was smiling now. "That's perfect. Let's put the Beach Boys on."

Jennifer asked, "Please tell me you two aren't actually going to start singing."

As they crept forward in traffic, *Surfin' USA* started emanating from the Jeep's speakers. And Tom and Stephen did in fact join Mike Love, the Wilson brothers and Al

Jardine. "If everybody had an ocean across the USA, then everybody'd be surfin' like Californi-a..."

Jen laughed, and then joined Stephen and Tom in singing along.

Stephen didn't care how long the rest of the drive would take to their Manhattan hotel.

Chapter 3

Stephen and Jennifer had an early check in at The Ian-Soho Hotel. The 5-star Ian was a unique 21-story, 206-room building that generated descriptions among guests like bright, clean, and modern. Their room offered custom-made furniture, more space than typical Manhattan hotels, and expansive windows offering arresting views of the Hudson River.

Jennifer remarked, "Well, staying here for three nights certainly beats riding back and forth on the Long Island Railroad or the L.I.E. each day."

Stephen moved next to her, closed his green eyes, breathed in deeply, and then looked out at part of the city, the river, and New Jersey on the other side of the water. "Agreed."

Jennifer said, "We can enjoy this more later. We've already missed at least a couple of today's matches. Shall we head over to the tournament?"

"Sounds good."

The couple made sure they had what was needed for a day of watching beach volleyball, including the lanyards housing V.I.P. tickets supplied by Maggie Stone. Tom and Maggie, along with some of the volleyball players, including Melissa Ambler, were also staying at The Ian. With Maggie having a room, Tom already had journeyed over to Pier 26, where the two-court beach volleyball stadium had been set up.

After a short walk and with their special tickets, Jennifer and Stephen breezed onto the pier. Various booths were setup seemingly offering almost anything for sale that related to the beach, the sun, and volleyball, as well as a wide array of beverages and foods. As they strolled closer to the stands and court, the music grew louder from enormous speakers below a giant video screen on the northside of the courts. The stands were on the east and west sides of the courts, while at sand level, tables with umbrellas ran in front of each stand and along the south side of the playing area.

As he and Jennifer emerged from one of the tunnels running underneath the stands, Stephen could immediately feel the atmosphere that Melissa had created. It was electric and laid back at the same time. As he glanced at the matches being played on the two courts in front of him, Stephen thought about the athletic prowess, intensity and competition unfolding against the backdrop of a beach party.

That's pro sports. Fans enjoying themselves while watching excellence courtesy of professional athletes. But still, this entire scene takes it to another level. Men and women playing in bathing suits on sand. The music.

Jennifer and Stephen followed a young man in a "Bedlam on the Beach" red polo shirt, khaki shorts and no shoes.

No shoes? Stephen looked around a bit more, and saw that all staff on the sand wore polo shirts and shorts, while lacking shoes.

Jennifer looked back at Stephen, and with a smile, said, "I love this."

They were shown to their table, which sat at the back of the women's court in the south corner. The brown-haired, dark-eyed staffer pulled a chair out for Jennifer, and then announced, "I hope this table works well?"

Stephen replied, "Yes, thanks very much."

"You're welcome. Of course, with your V.I.P package, all food and drinks, including alcoholic beverages, are complimentary. Whenever you need anything, just wave me down or anyone else dressed this way."

This time both Jennifer and Stephen replied, "Thanks."

The early-twenty-something, smiling staff person then asked, "What can I get you now? Perhaps a drink?"

Jennifer smiled at Stephen, and then replied, "I'd like a piña colada?"

"Of course, and you, sir?"

Stephen answered, "Make it two."

"Great. I'll be right back."

Stephen looked at Jennifer, taking in his wife's beauty – her fair skin, slightly upturned nose, short, dark auburn hair, and deep brown eyes. *Lucky man.* He said, "I think I'm going to enjoy the next few days."

Before Jennifer could respond, out of the corner of his eye, Stephen spotted a volleyball heading in their direction. He reached up and tapped the ball in flight, stopping its progress and knocking it about two feet straight up in the air. As it started to come down, he grabbed it.

Jennifer observed, "Nice."

"Apparently, we might be in on some of the action courtside." He turned to toss the ball back, and was taken off guard as he recognized the tall blond-haired woman in a red bikini waiting for the white-and-yellow ball to be tossed back. Stephen saw a mirrored look of recognition in Jessica West's eyes.

He casually tossed the ball back, and West merely responded, "Thanks."

Jennifer's mouth was open slightly. She started to talk in a low voice. "Stephen..."

Stephen reached out his hand, and placed it on Jennifer's. He casually nodded. Stephen maintained his relaxed look, while meeting his wife's eyes. He could see that Jennifer arrived at the understanding that discussing the fact that Jessica West was playing in this tournament might have to wait until a more private moment.

Stephen then noted that West's playing partner was another CDM employee, Brooke Semmler. He reached into a pocket of his cargo-style shorts, and pulled out a pair of sunglasses. Stephen slipped them on, and instinctively began to more closely scan the rest of his surroundings. Additional familiar faces jumped out at him.

On the west side of the court, standing behind the tables and up against the base of the stands, was a woman wearing tan shorts, a green polo shirt, sunglasses and a baseball-style cap.

Paige.

A male figure mirrored Paige on the opposite side of the playing area.

Chase Axelrod.

The piña coladas arrived. Stephen drew up some of the icy drink through the straw. He then spotted a man descending one of the sets of stairs in the east stands. His light blue linen shirt was a bit rumpled, while the same could be said about his moustache.

Charlie. Geez, Grant, you're getting sloppy. Took you long enough to ID familiar faces.

Stephen started to lean over to talk to Jennifer, but he halted, spotting another face he knew at one of the tables across the men's court. The individual, about Stephen's age, had removed his sunglasses to briefly rub his eyes. Stephen worked to gain additional focus, which confirmed the identification.

My old Mossad friend, Elon Mizrah. Well, that makes things even more interesting.

Stephen looked at Jennifer, and asked, "Did I say that I was going to enjoy the next few days?"

Chapter 4

While watching Jessica West and Brooke Semmler play a competitive match, with the CDM duo winning in a third set, Stephen continued to scan the area. He didn't recognize any other faces.

It was expected that none of the CDM people acknowledged him or Jennifer.

What's the job, and why the Mossad interest?

After the men's match being played next to West and Semmler's contest came to an end, twenty minutes were allocated for fans to find food, merchandise or the restrooms, while the teams playing in the upcoming pair of matches emerged to warm up on the sand. Not long after the next two matches got under way, Stephen leaned over to Jennifer and whispered, "I'm going to try to find out what this is all about."

"Okay." Jennifer added, "I'm going to order another piña colada. Want me to have one brought over for you?"

Stephen smiled. "Sure."

Jen keeping it in perspective.

Stephen strolled past the other tables, and stopped next to Paige Caldwell, similarly leaning his back to the base of the stands. Their shoulders lightly touched.

Paige didn't look at Stephen, but she smirked and quietly said, "Are you here for the young ladies in bikinis, Pastor Grant?"

He chose to ignore the needling, something that Paige had done since the two of them worked, and did much more, together at the CIA. Stephen simply said, "Hi, Paige. How are you?"

"Good. How about you?"

"Same." He paused to see if Paige might continue with the conversation. Since she fell quiet, he asked, "So, can I ask why the interest in beach volleyball? And along those same lines, does CDM have an intense volleyball training program now?"

Paige smiled while still watching her surroundings. "I guess I can give you a quick rundown." She leaned in closer to Stephen's ear. "Melissa Ambler, as you know, not only owns this Bedlam on the Beach tour, but she plays, and is partnered with Ranya Khan."

"Ranya Khan?"

"Not up on the list of up-and-coming beach volleyball players?"

"Apparently not."

The two varied the decibel of their conversation based on changes in the music and noise from the crowd.

Paige said, "Khan is the daughter of a Saudi prince."

Stephen interrupted, "Ah, Prince Hkim Khan?"

"Right."

"He's the one leading the charge to open up Saudi society, and while doing so, trying to isolate the Islamic militants."

"Right, again. Ranya Khan came to the U.S. to go to college, and she wound up becoming a top collegiate volleyball player. Since graduating, she's been pursuing professional beach volleyball."

"That probably doesn't go over well with those radicals her father is trying to isolate."

Paige smiled. "Hell, it doesn't go over well with her father, but he allows it. He's the one who hired us. The prince made it a requirement that if Ranya was going to school in America, she had to acquiesce to a bodyguard. She had one throughout four years at USC. But he knew that her playing beach volleyball would increase the risks. So, here we are. And Melissa was fine with the added protection."

"And Melissa's also fine with a CDM team on her tour?"

Paige shrugged. "Part of the deal. It gives us two people close to Ranya a lot of the time. Jessica actually played in college, and Brooke was passable. She was on her high school team."

"High school?"

"I know. But they haven't embarrassed themselves, and they're intensely competitive. The earlier match actually was their first win of the season, so I'm guessing the two of them are sky high right now, prepping for another match later."

"Nice." Stephen asked, "Is this the last tournament of the year?"

"One more in Boston in two weeks."

"And it's been quiet?"

Paige turned for the first time and looked at Stephen. He couldn't see her eyes behind the dark sunglasses, but was familiar with the general expression.

He asked, "What happened?"

Paige glanced around, and said, "Let's just say there was an incident in May in Manhattan Beach. It was reported as something different."

Stephen nodded.

Apparently, Paige and Company foiled some kind of attack.

"Given the Saudi prince factor, I guess that explains why Mossad is here."

Once again, Paige turned and looked directly at Stephen. "Mossad?"

Chapter 5

"Why does he call himself '11'? Why not come forward to us, at least?" A dozen of the thirteen other men crammed into a dirty, four-room apartment in Brooklyn nodded in agreement.

The thirteenth man, Mostafa Ruhani, who led the cell, shook his head. "Don't be a fool. What if 11 had been exposed to the three in California?"

"What's the difference? They're dead," came the response.

Ruhani sighed. "I know that. But if any had survived, 11 would have been put at risk."

The complainer continued, "I suppose. But I don't like it."

Ruhani turned on the man. "You don't like it! What else do you not like?"

The protestor sat up a bit straighter on the edge of one of the two beds. "Well, why are we instructed to not even injure the whore daughter of Prince Khan? After all, she's the example of what happens when we stray from the teachings of the prophet and Allah. She is the one who should be punished first, and for all to see."

The twelve who had backed him previously now exhibited nervousness and discomfort. Each averted their eyes from the ongoing exchange.

Ruhani leaned forward in his chair. "I see. So, you now understand everything that is going on here, and wish to lead the cause. Is that the case?" The normal look etched on Ruhani's face would never be described as friendly. Indeed, it was quite the opposite. His sharp nose, thin lips, sunken cheeks, and close-cut beard and black hair, peppered with bits of gray, gave him a severe look. But then there were the eyes. While narrow, the display of intense anger was unmistakable. Few wanted to return his stare for more than a few seconds.

That was the case now. The man voicing protests lowered his head and fell silent. The others exhibited no desire to take up his line of questioning.

Ruhani continued to stare at his men – moving those eyes from person to person.

The man who had raised questions now relented. "Of course not, Mostafa. I beg your forgiveness."

Ruhani continued to offer a withering stare. He finally appeared satisfied, and then continued relaying the instructions he had received from 11 via email.

His men listened closely, with respect and fear.

Chapter 6

The first day's matches at the Bedlam on the Beach Tour's New York Open had ended under the lights a little after eight. Nearly an hour later, Tom and Maggie Stone were having dinner with Melissa Ambler in the restaurant sitting atop the Ian-Soho Hotel.

Over drinks and salad, Maggie and Melissa reviewed the first day's action, both on the sand and on the business end of things.

After salad plates were removed, Tom asked Melissa, "How are you managing to juggle all of this?"

Melissa took a sip of water, and then replied, "What do you mean?"

Tom smiled. "Melissa, we're your friends and I'm the priest at your parish. I just want to make sure you're okay. After all, as far as I know, you're running Corevana and the education foundation. You not only own this volleyball tour, but you're also playing. Oh yeah, and then there's getting back to modeling and the baseball league. To most humans, that sounds like it might be a bit overwhelming."

Melissa offered a guarded response. "I'm doing fine."

Tom and Maggie glanced at each other, and then Tom added, "I hope so. We also haven't seen you at St. Bart's in a while?"

Relief crossed Melissa's face as the entrees arrived.

The waiter asked if anything more was needed. Tom replied, "Thank you. I think we're fine. Everything looks delicious."

While Maggie and Tom moved to take initial forkfuls from their respective dishes, Melissa looked up from the table. On this clear night with a light breeze, she turned her gaze to the south to the lit-up Freedom Tower. She sighed and sat back. Still looking up, Melissa observed, "Tom, when you said grace earlier, that was the first time I had prayed in probably several weeks."

Tom asked, "Why? Is there something wrong?"

"I'm not sure. My lack of prayer, and going to church less and less haven't exactly been conscious, purposeful decisions. It's just kind of happened."

Tom paused, and then commented, "Well, that's good, at least?"

Both Maggie and Melissa offered him looks of surprise.

He smiled. "What I mean is that this isn't a conscious decision. You know, it's not like you decided that you're mad at the Church or God, and you're done with Him."

"No, that's not it."

"Good."

Each took a bite of their respective dinners. Tom was chewing on a piece of pan-seared New York Strip Steak with a garlic butter sauce. Maggie chose bacon-wrapped sea scallops in a sweet teriyaki sauce, while Melissa had a kale pesto chicken and pasta dish.

Tom asked Melissa, "Do you want to talk about this now?"

She swallowed, and simply said, "I don't know. Maybe."

After more chewing of food, Tom said, "Okay. Well, what are possible excuses for not coming to church?"

Melissa hesitated, and then answered, "I'm not really sure."

"Does it have to do with Mike?"

Melissa shifted slightly in her seat, and then shook her head. "That wouldn't make any sense. After all, I'm running his company and our foundation now, and keeping our baseball team going."

Maggie nodded, and continued eating while her husband and Melissa talked.

Tom said, "Right. But was there something different about you and Mike with church?"

Melissa moved items around on her plate, while Tom and Maggie took bites of food.

After nearly a minute, Melissa looked back up at Tom and Maggie with newly moistened eyes. Maggie reached out to rest her own hand on her friend's. Melissa replied with a smile, while a tear escaped her left eye. As she quickly wiped it away, tears began to form in Maggie's eyes as well.

Melissa took a deep breath, and said, "I don't want to talk about this."

Tom said, "I understand."

Melissa and Maggie returned to their plans for the coming three days of the tournament.

At the end of the main course, Melissa said, "Do you two mind if I head up to my room? I've got to get serious rest before tomorrow. I'm getting some Corevana people in California up at an ungodly hour for a conference call early in the morning, and then I have to get ready for the second day of the tournament."

Maggie said, "Of course not. Go."

Tom added, "No worries."

Melissa said, "Stay where you are. Enjoy some dessert. I've got the meal covered already." She stood up, came over to Maggie, kissed her on the cheek, and said, "Thanks for all you're doing."

"You're welcome. Thank you."

Tom rose to his feet. Melissa leaned in and gave him a peck on the cheek as well. She lingered, and whispered, "Please don't give up on me."

Tom replied, "Of course not. Never."

Chapter 7

"This is a freakin' weird case," observed Charlie Driessen. "It is," agreed Paige Caldwell. She added, "It's also been one of our most profitable."

Driessen smiled. "Yeah, well, there's that."

While the Stones were dining with Melissa Ambler, Caldwell and Driessen were standing at the bar in a trendy Greenwich Village restaurant, nursing non-alcoholic drinks. Their experience allowed them to fit in anywhere, so a Manhattan bar was easy. Driessen even tamed his unruly mustache and thin hair, while upgrading his wardrobe to an ironed light blue button-down shirt and tan slacks with a crisp crease – far from his typically rumpled look. Meanwhile, Caldwell's light gray cargo-style Capri pants and white lace top fashionably highlighted her freckles, athleticism and strength.

Caldwell and Driessen were keeping an eye on Ranya Khan, who was having dinner with Anthony Deluca, her longtime boyfriend from USC. Deluca was a generally good-looking guy – average build with dark hair, thick eyebrows and a wide smile – and the son of a wealthy supermarket CEO.

At the other end of the bar, a man in a dark suit with a thin black tie was doing the same thing as Caldwell and Driessen. Hamza Alam served as Ranya Khan's personal bodyguard.

Throughout the Bedlam on the Beach volleyball season, the CDM team was well aware of Alam, and vice versa. But when Caldwell reached out at the start of the tour to see how they might work together, Alam quickly rebuffed her. Caldwell's subsequent appeal to Prince Khan resulted in basically being told to leave Alam alone, and do your own work. And that's how it had gone.

"Is there trouble in paradise?" asked Driessen as he looked at the couple sitting at a table no more than 30 feet away.

The body language between Ranya and Anthony had changed. Ranya's expression had intensified, with a cold expression and short sentences coming in bursts. Ranya's eyes also avoided Anthony's.

Caldwell commented, "It looks like it."

According to Driessen over the last three-or-so months, Deluca always seemed to have a "dopey, I'm-in-love look." Now, Deluca wore a look of shock – a mix of sadness and anger.

Caldwell added, "She's dumping him."

"Ya think?"

Driessen and Caldwell watched as Deluca became increasingly agitated while listening to Ranya. She finished a sentence with a shrug of the shoulders, and then sat back in her chair.

Deluca lowered his head, staring at the linen napkin on his lap. And then he jumped to his feet, knocking his chair back into the person sitting behind him at another table. He pointed at Ranya, and yelled, "You bitch! After everything, you just say it's over. I don't think..."

He was interrupted by a strong hand grabbing hold of his left arm. Once Deluca had jumped to his feet, Hamza Alam had moved into action.

Deluca tried to pull his arm away from Alam, but the bodyguard's grip was vice-like. Alam pulled Deluca closer, and whispered, "Anthony, my friend, I urge you to keep your voice down and to not do anything you might regret."

Caldwell and Driessen simply watched. They had no reason – at least, not yet – to get involved.

Deluca struggled harder against Alam's grip, and said, "Get your fucking hands off of me."

Alam actually tightened his hold. He added, "Do you understand, Anthony?"

Deluca looked at Ranya, who was calmly watching all of this develop from her seat. As he turned back to Alam, Deluca gave up the struggle. "Yes, I understand."

"Good. Thank you, Anthony." Alam slowly released Deluca.

Anthony Deluca then looked around to see that nearly everyone in the restaurant was staring at him. He bit his lip, turned and walked out.

Alam looked down at Ranya Khan. She nodded. Alam took money out of his pocket, and deposited enough on the tablecloth to more than cover the dinner bill. Ranya then led the way out of the restaurant, with Alam following. Neither one even glanced as they passed by Caldwell and Driessen.

After they exited, Driessen added to the cash they left on the bar, and he and Caldwell moved toward the front door. As they walked, Driessen asked, "Did you see the look on her face? That was nasty cold."

"Maybe Deluca deserved it," replied Caldwell.

Driessen shook his head slightly, but said, "Yeah, maybe."

Chapter 8

While Ranya Khan was exiting the restaurant in the Village and after the Stones had descended from their rooftop meal at the Ian-Soho Hotel, Stephen and Jennifer Grant remained seated *al fresco* in front of a small restaurant in Little Italy. They had just finished their main courses, and were now debating whether or not to have dessert.

Jennifer said, "I've eaten way too much today, but the tiramisu is supposed to be delicious here. How about we split it?"

"Sounds good to me."

Jennifer smiled and started to respond, but stopped. She saw Stephen's eyes wander across the street. Looking in the same direction, Jennifer asked, "What is it?"

"I'm not sure, but..." He paused, and then said, "Yes, that's him."

"Who?"

Earlier in the dinner, Stephen had quietly updated Jennifer on what Paige had passed along as to why the CDM team was on hand, including Jessica and Brooke actually competing in beach volleyball. Stephen also provided a quick rundown on Elon Mizrah.

It was Mizrah who had just stepped from the street onto the sidewalk, and now moved between the large potted plants that served as a barrier between restaurant-goers at tables and New Yorkers walking by. If the Mossad operative stood out for anything, it would be his averageness. His brown hair, with traces of gray, was cut in a neat, nondistinctive manner. His five-foot-eight-inch frame was neither skinny, nor weighty. And his facial features were forgettable, with a slightly undersized nose and eyes that, if one looked close, seemed to be a bit too far apart. He wore faded jeans and an untucked, short-sleeve checkered shirt. Without hesitation, he pulled out the one empty chair at the Grants' table and sat down. Mizrah smiled at Stephen. He extended his hand to Jennifer, and said, "Hello, I'm Elon Mizrah, an old friend of your husband's."

Jennifer shook his hand, smiled, and said, "It's nice to meet you. Stephen's told me about you."

Mizrah raised a mocking eyebrow, looked at Stephen, and said, "Has he now?"

Stephen smiled, and said, "It's good to see you, Elon. How are you?"

"I am well, my friend. How long has it been since we last saw each other?" He paused, and contorted his face like he was trying to solve a difficult math problem. "Twenty ... no, could it be 25 years?"

"Something like that."

"And you're a pastor now!" He chuckled. "That's amusing. I would not have predicted it, especially when we were with those two women in..."

Stephen interrupted, "Well, we all change."

Mizrah said, "Oh, yes, of course." He looked at Jennifer and said, "I apologize. That was long before he met you, of course, Dr. Grant."

He knows when Jen and I met and that she is a Ph.D. economist. Have Elon and Mossad been keeping tabs?

Jennifer said, "We all have histories. And please, it's Jennifer."

"Yes, yes, and you must call me Elon." He turned back to Stephen, and commented, "Stephen, I must say that over the last few years, at least, you've seen some action not typical for an American Lutheran pastor. Or at least, I assume it's not typical."

"Yes, well..."

Elon leaned in closer, and interrupted in a whisper, "My friend, I think your body count in a collar might rival or even surpass what you accomplished with the CIA."

There's my answer. Keeping tabs on me, which is not all that surprising, I suppose.

Mizrah continued, "That was a shame what happened to Pope Augustine..."

Time to shift the focus. Stephen interrupted, "What have you been up to, Elon?"

Mizrah smiled ruefully. "Ah, yes, you say that we all change. Perhaps, perhaps not. My work continues."

Fortunately, the table next to them was empty, and the street noise served as a convenient cover for their conversation.

Stephen knew the answer, but nonetheless asked, "I see. So, why does Mossad have you hanging out at a beach volleyball tournament in Manhattan?"

Before an answer could be offered, the waitress arrived at the table, looking a bit bewildered at the arrival of a third diner. She looked at Mizrah, and said, "Oh, hello. Um, would you like a menu?"

Mizrah smiled, and shook his head. "I'm sorry. I just saw my friends and sat down." He looked at Stephen and asked, "You were about to order dessert?"

Stephen said, "Yes, we were."

Mizrah declared, "Then I will simply join in on dessert."

Stephen replied, "Of course, that would be great." He turned to the waitress, and indicating that he was ordering for Jennifer and himself, said, "We're going to split your tiramisu and have two cappuccinos."

The waitress volunteered, "Great choice."

"I will do the same then," said Mizrah. "But I'm not sharing mine."

The waitress laughed, and off she went to put in the orders.

Stephen said, "The least I can do for an old friend is buy you dessert."

"Thank you."

"Again, why are you and Mossad interested in American beach volleyball?"

Mizrah answered mockingly, "Stephen, perhaps I love the sport, and am here on my own."

Stephen and Jennifer each raised an eyebrow at his response.

Looking back and forth at each, Mizrah said, "You two definitely are married." He chuckled at his own observation, and then continued, "Okay, it's simple, and I'm sure you already know the answer. Israel likes what Prince Khan is trying to do in Saudi Arabia, and after what happened in California, I'm here to help keep an eye on Ranya Khan." He paused. "It's like I'm helping the Saudis and that security firm owned by your old Agency friends, Paige Caldwell and Charlie Driessen, along with Sean McEnany. McEnany is a more recent friend and a parishioner at your church, right?"

Stephen simply nodded, while Jennifer could not hide her look of surprise.

Mizrah added, "And I'm here without them even knowing it. Although, I'm sure they're informed now, since you spotted me at the event earlier today."

Stephen replied, "Yes, I mentioned it to Paige Caldwell."

Mizrah leaned back in his chair, and simply said, "Right. Although I wasn't involved, Caldwell and Company have done some work for us."

"Not surprising."

Mizrah sighed. "So, Paige Caldwell."

Will he go there?

"That's got to be a little weird."

"Meaning?"

"Well, you become a pastor, leaving the CIA, and Paige, behind. But then she's back, you're married, and given the history..."

Jennifer interjected, "If I'm not concerned, Elon, then I'm sure you need not be."

Mizrah laughed robustly. "I know. I'm just needling my old friend. I apologize, Jennifer."

Jennifer smiled and said, "Yes, of course."

Jen's not sure about Elon. Can't decide if she likes him or not. I'll have to reassure her later.

The desserts and cappuccinos arrived, and the three began to partake.

Stephen asked, "So, Elon, what brought you to our table tonight?"

He shrugged. "To be honest, I wanted to meet the woman who married Stephen Grant, and was just looking to catch up with an old friend."

Stephen looked Mizrah in the eyes and smiled. Over the next hour, they did, in fact, catch up. Mizrah spoke about his family. Stephen knew Mizrah's wife, who was a former Mossad operative, but their three children and two grandchildren were news to him. He could see the joy in Mizrah's eyes when speaking of the children and grandchildren. This old Mossad colleague also clearly was fascinated by the life that Stephen had carved out as a pastor, and enjoyed hearing about how he and Jennifer got together, as well as her work and travel.

Stephen could tell that by the end of the conversation, Jennifer needed no convincing on Elon Mizrah. He had won her over.

Chapter 9

Jennifer and Stephen woke up early on Friday morning. Jennifer decided that she was going to take full advantage of the hotel's health club, while Stephen went for a run.

It had been some time since he had the opportunity for a run in Manhattan.

The sun was rising, but the hour was still early enough that the activity of the finance industry had not yet ramped up. And for a day in August, the humidity was low, which gave Grant a little extra boost.

Dressed in a Cincinnati Reds t-shirt, tan shorts and white running shoes, Grant made a left on Canal Street; eventually a right onto Broadway; and then proceeded to avoid a few pedestrians, and a vehicle here and there.

A man coming out of a coffee shop spotted Grant's shirt, and called out, "The freakin' Reds. Are you kiddin' me? They suck."

Grant smiled and waved. *Ah, New York.*

He made his way down to Trinity Church and the grave of Alexander Hamilton. Making a quick left onto Wall Street, Federal Hall came up on his left.

How many people really think of lower Manhattan as a place rich in history?

Grant turned right onto Broad Street, dashing by the New York Stock Exchange. He proceeded to weave his way through short, narrow streets, and then turned his path back north.

He was on Greenwich Street, with the 9-11 Memorial coming up on his left. The terrorist attacks on September 11, 2001, came shortly after Grant had been ordained at St. Mary's Lutheran Church. That day and for a time afterward registered as the only period when he seriously questioned becoming a pastor. The pull to return to the CIA had been strong.

I didn't intend on winding up here this morning – at least not consciously.

Grant slowed to a walk, and then moved under the trees, approaching one of the two massive footprints where the World Trade Center, the Twin Towers, formerly stood. The names of those murdered on that day were listed around the edges. Water streamed down the sides into a lower pool, and finally farther into a hole in the center, with people around the memorial unable to see the bottom.

Grant stopped in front of the etched names, and looked around.

Not too many people at this hour. It's before the crowds arrive, when, unfortunately, too many individuals and groups ignore or fail to understand the sacredness of such a place, missing the idea that quiet shows respect. Stop it, Grant. Not the time. Be generous.

He breathed deeply and took in his surroundings. Grant thought about events he personally had been involved in after the 9-11 horrors – more attacks on the city tied in with the assassination of a pope; the Long Island minor league baseball murders, including the loss of Mike Vanacore; and the recent terrorist assault on churches, here in New York and across the nation; and more.

Grant closed his eyes and lowered his head.

Dear Lord, thank you for all you've done for me and for all. For sending your Son to take on and wipe away our sins through the cross. For His offering of forgiveness, redemption and salvation. Lord, I stand at a most solemn place that makes clear the ills of this fallen world, the deep sinfulness of human nature. I know that You were here on that day in 2001, alongside all being struck down, injured and working to help others. We take comfort, I take comfort, knowing that You understand our many and varied sufferings in this life, and that thanks to Jesus, sin, suffering and death have been conquered.

He opened his eyes, and scanned the many names carved before him.

Lord, please be with the family and friends of the victims of this atrocity these years later. And open the hearts and minds of all who come to this place.

Grant took a deep breath, and began walking slowly alongside the memorial.

And I pray that individuals and groups around the world planning and carrying out evil in the name of religion have their hard hearts softened, their minds opened, their ignorance remedied, and their hatred wiped away. All of this can only be accomplished because of and thanks to You.

He stopped, leaned forward, and traced some of the names with his hands.

I pray all of this in the name of Jesus.

Grant straightened up, turned and began walking back to Greenwich Street. Once there, he returned to his morning run, heading back to the hotel and Jennifer.

Chapter 10

By late Friday morning, Jennifer and Stephen were back courtside, with Tom Stone joining them. Maggie, of course, was running around working at the event.

On the double court, a women's match had just finished, and the men's was concluding.

Serving match point, one of the tallest men on the Bedlam tour tossed the ball in the air, jumped and launched a cross-court serve. No chance for a return existed, as it fell just inside the sideline.

After the cheering died down following a brief celebration on the sand, the courtside digital clock started a 20-minute countdown to the next two matches. The music rose to thundering levels.

This was the first chance that Tom, Jennifer and Stephen had to chat since the ride into the city.

Stephen asked, "How was dinner with Melissa?"

While all three at the table wore shorts, Stephen had donned a casual yellow button-down shirt and Jennifer a light pink polo. As for Tom, his longtime preference for wearing Hawaiian-style shirts had flourished in a beach volleyball setting. Right now, he sported a faded blue floral shirt.

Tom responded, "We generally had a nice dinner. That restaurant on the top floor of our hotel is excellent. You two should try it before leaving town."

Stephen and Jennifer nodded.

Tom continued, "Anyway, Maggie and I had a talk with Melissa, but there's more to ... work on, let's just say."

Stephen took the signal, and replied, "Fair enough."

Jennifer added, "Let us know if we can help."

Tom said, "Prayers are good."

Their attention turned to the courts as the four teams hit the sand to warm up for their matches.

Tom leaned forward when he recognized one of the players. He turned to Stephen, and whispered, "Hey, isn't that...?"

Stephen answered, "Yes, it is. But I can't really go into it."

Tom hesitated, and then said, "Okay. Anything I should be concerned about?"

"Unlikely."

Tom's stare lingered on Stephen.

Meanwhile, since arriving, Stephen had been scanning the crowd nearly as much as he had been watching volleyball.

They were interrupted by a waiter. It was the same person as the previous day, again in a red polo shirt, khaki shorts and no shoes. He took their lunch order.

The two matches began at the same time. Given his southern California experience with the sport and an upbeat personality that often led him to sharing his enthusiasms, Tom proceeded to supply a kind of rolling commentary on the action, in particular, the women's match, given that all three at the table knew Jessica West.

It was clear that both Jennifer and Stephen enjoyed listening to Tom's more-or-less play by play, peppering him with a few questions along the way.

Deeper into the match, Tom observed, "You can tell that Jessica has experience. She's really good, showing strong instincts and skills, and that rare knack for making her playing partner better. She not only gets to balls that many others can't, but manages to set her partner so that they have a real opportunity to score. Impressive. If she stuck with this, she could be a top player."

Stephen simply replied, "That's interesting."

That doesn't surprise me. Jessica is disciplined and determined. I wonder if she might be tempted to walk away from the CDM life and try something like this. I'd be surprised given her focus on doling out justice after the deaths of her father, brother and fiancé. Although, she showed another side, or maybe a re-emerging side, when I flew with CDM to Russia. She enjoyed the Vikings in the Super Bowl, and sharing her fandom with Phil Lucena.

Stone continued with his assessment of the Semmler-West team. "As for Semmler, it's really about raw athleticism, from what I can see. She's fast, including very quick reaction times, and she can get some air. But her inexperience is pretty clear. Again, West makes her better."

When Brooke and Jessica won the match in two sets, with Brooke setting Jessica up for a spike that went untouched by their opponents, everyone seemed surprised, except Tom.

As they were standing and applauding, Tom looked back and forth at Stephen and Jennifer. "Like I said, Jessica West really is good."

Stephen realized that while West and Semmler were competing on the sand, his focus had tilted heavily toward the volleyball and away from scanning the crowd. Although, he already had identified the familiar faces, namely, the CDM trio of Paige Caldwell, Charlie Driessen, and Chase Axelrod, along with Elon Mizrah.

At the conclusion of a three-set men's match, fans moved in and out of the stadium during the break. The next contest on the women's court featured the team of Melissa Ambler and Ranya Khan. The entrance of that pair brought the ever-looming presence of Hamza Alam standing off the court, not far from Paige Caldwell. Caldwell looked at Alam. He didn't return the glance.

Meanwhile, new arrivals in the stands included Anthony Deluca on the west side, and Mostafa Ruhani on the east. Two other members of Ruhani's cell were seated elsewhere as well. As the contest began, Deluca's expression never ranged from a simmering anger. Ruhani watched with dispassion. However, while Deluca watched Ranya, Ruhani took little notice of the volleyball.

As for Caldwell's team, they took note of Deluca. Ruhani's presence, though, failed to earn recognition.

From his own courtside seat, Elon Mizrah was looking past the men's contest in front of him to keep an eye on Ambler and Khan, as well as glancing in the direction of Alam and the CDM team members.

An hour and a half after the first serve, Ambler and Khan won in a 15-13 third set. While everyone stood with the victory, Deluca didn't join in the cheering and applause. Meanwhile, Ruhani offered perfunctory clapping while scanning everything going on off the court. His two followers did the same.

Chapter 11

At the urging of Paige Caldwell, Brooke Semmler and Kent Holtwick had left the Secret Service and the White House behind to join CDM International Strategies and Security. That move not only provided a substantial boost to Semmler and Holtwick's take home pay, but also to their relationship.

Caldwell, Driessen and McEnany were pleased with the addition of the two 29-year-olds to the firm. Both possessed excellent field skills. In addition, Semmler offered encyclopedic knowledge of the international political landscape, while Holtwick's expertise in finance, built during college and earning an MBA, was proving handy. And as their relationship moved out of the shadows, they were diligent in making sure that it created no issues in their new workplace.

On the same floor of the Ian-Soho Hotel as their rooms, CDM had secured a conference room. Around the clear table, seated in black, high-back chairs were Caldwell, Driessen, Axelrod, Semmler and West. The five were in the midst of a lively, Friday night conversation.

Driessen asked, "So, Paige didn't list playing beach volleyball as one of the perks of joining CDM?"

Semmler's blue eyes sparkled, as did her smile. She laughed, and ran her right hand through light brown hair. "No. This is not exactly what I expected. And while I get why we're here, this has been incredibly fun." She looked at her playing partner, Jessica West, sitting to her right.

West added, "Yeah, I think we've got a real chance to play on Sunday." For both the men and women's tournaments, the semifinals and finals were scheduled for Sunday. She continued, "When we get back to our room, Brooke and I are going to watch tape on Kelsey Gale and Sunny Sackett. They're obviously supposed to beat us tomorrow, but they're vulnerable. We're going to finish plotting out how to exploit their weaknesses."

West stopped talking as everyone else around the table was watching her in silence.

Driessen commented, "No one can say that you haven't embraced your role on this assignment."

West's look of determination melted in sheepishness. "Oh, right, sorry."

Caldwell was smiling. "It's not a problem, Jessica. I get it. Just try to keep an eye out for any bad guys."

"Yeah ... well .. of course."

That generated some laughs around the table, with even the taciturn Chase Axelrod breaking into a smile.

Caldwell added, "With you two" – she indicated West and Semmler – "actually playing tomorrow, and possibly Sunday, Sean is going to join us early tomorrow morning to help cover the weekend."

Driessen said, "Sean McEnany at a beach volleyball tournament. That's probably a first."

"Thanks for that insight, Charlie. Anyone else have anything of value to add?" Other than Driessen grunting in response to the jab, no one responded. Caldwell continued, "Okay. Brooke, I assume you'll be speaking with Kent?"

Semmler replied, "Yes."

"Can you just give him an update on our conversation?"

"Sure."

Caldwell looked at Jessica. "And can you let Phil know?"

"Of course." West added, "In fact, unless we've got something else, I'm going to call him now, before Brooke and I get lost in video and strategy."

Caldwell replied, "Go ahead. We're basically done."

West left, and walked down the hallway to the hotel room that she and Brooke were sharing. She closed the door, pulled out her phone, and called Phil Lucena.

Lucena answered, "Jess, you and Brooke were incredible today. Congratulations."

West smiled, and said, "Thanks, babe. I think we have a real shot at playing on Sunday."

"That would be fantastic."

"How are you feeling?"

"I made some nice strides again today at PT, and I'm not tired at all. My stamina is improving."

After tumbling over the side of the Manhattan Beach Pier, Lucena hit the sand hard and awkwardly, with the fall made worse as the terrorist's body landed on him. Lucena suffered a shattered right collar bone, a cracked upper spine, and a severe head contusion. He had to be operated on immediately, and wound up in a coma for nearly a week. When he awoke, Jessica was at his bedside. Since Phil's injury, Jessica had been jumping between her Bedlam on the Beach assignment and helping Phil with his recovery. In fact, she played a big part in urging him on, and getting him home. It was a natural step, both agreed, for Jessica to move into Phil's small home.

Phil proceeded with his recovery update, and then Jessica brought him up to speed as to what was going on with the CDM assignment.

After twenty minutes, Phil said, "I could go on talking, but I know that you and Brooke need to get to planning for tomorrow's match."

"I'd like to keep talking as well..."

"No, get focused on your game."

"Thanks, Phil."

"You're thanking me? You've done everything for me. Without you, I would not be where I am now."

"Well, you know, I love you."

Phil smiled broadly on the other end of the call. "I love you as well, and by the way, I will never get tired of hearing you say that."

"Same here."

Phil added, "And if you're not aware, the announcers constantly talk about how good you are on the court."

"Are you going to bring this up again?"

"I know how much you love playing, but I also know how much you care about what we're doing at CDM. But just think about what you want to do after the Boston stop. You have wonderful options, and I want you to be happy and have no regrets. And you know that whatever you choose, I'll support you."

Jessica said, "I know. Thanks."

Just as they finished the call, Brooke knocked and entered the room. She asked, "Ready?"

Jessica nodded, and replied, "Let's figure out how to win tomorrow."

Chapter 12

While Brooke Semmler and Jessica West started reviewing the opposition, Melissa Ambler and Ranya Khan were doing the same one floor down.

As they assessed strengths and weaknesses watching video in Ambler's room, the objective was to find something that might have been missed before, something they could work to their advantage. But neither one seemed pleased with their progress.

Ambler, sitting cross legged on one of the beds, asked, "Is everything okay? You seem distracted."

Khan replied, "Yeah, I know." She was sitting in a chair with her bare feet resting on the other bed. "Tony and I broke up."

"Wow. You two were seeing each other for a long time, right?"

"Nearly four years."

"I'm sorry."

"Don't be. It was my idea. He was making me feel uncomfortable, very controlling."

"Really?"

A flash of anger crossed Khan's face. "What does that mean?"

Ambler leaned back. "Nothing. I didn't mean anything. It's just that he never struck me as being that way."

Khan's look went expressionless. She said, "People aren't always what they seem to be."

Ambler nodded, and added, "Is there anything I can do?"

Khan shook her head, and said, "Besides, it seems like I'm not the only one distracted?"

"True. I had dinner with two friends last night, and it got me thinking about what I've been neglecting."

"You seem to be involved in everything. What could you be neglecting?"

"To be honest, I was reminded that my spiritual life is not what it was. Not long after Mike was murdered, I slowly began drifting away from going to church. It's strange because our faith was so central to who we were..." Her voice trailed off.

In a matter-of-fact tone, Khan replied, "Maybe that was a different stage of your life. Maybe you've moved on."

Ambler was clearly surprised by her partner's response. "What?"

"You know. We all go through stages, and then find new paths."

"What an odd response."

"Really? How so?"

Ambler stared in disbelief. "Never mind. I shouldn't have brought it up. We need to get back to prepping for tomorrow."

Khan replied, "I'm with you on that."

As the video restarted on the wall-mounted television screen, Ambler initially glanced at her playing partner with annoyance in her eyes. Eventually, she re-focused on beach volleyball, and discussing an updated strategy.

Chapter 13

Stephen Grant's iPhone rumbled on the nightstand next to the hotel bed. The lit-up screen offered no information about the caller, but it did reveal that it was 2:35 in the morning.

Blocked call.

Grant sat up and answered in a whisper. "Hello?"

"Stephen, it's Elon. I apologize for waking you."

"It's okay. What's going on?"

"I hate to ask you this, but can you come over to my hotel?"

"Elon, now?"

"I know, I know. Again, I apologize. But I need you to look at something. And it has to be now. Stephen, I would not impose like this if it were not important."

"Okay. But where are you?"

It turned out that Elon Mizrah had a room at a hotel a block-and-a-half away from the Ian-Soho.

Stephen said, "Alright. I need to get dressed. I'll be there in 25 minutes."

"Perfect. Thank you, my friend."

After the call ended, Jennifer rolled over and said, "And what did your Mossad buddy want?"

"I'm sorry. He wants me to come over to his hotel now to look at something. He said it was important."

As Stephen got out of bed, he pledged not to be long, noting where Mizrah's hotel was. Jennifer remained silent while he got dressed – putting on a pair of jeans and a tan polo shirt. As he tied the laces on his sneakers, Stephen looked at his wife. He asked, "What is it?"

She sighed. "Please, be careful. I have a bad feeling about this."

Stephen smiled, and replied, "Well, since I can see you're actually worried, I'll refrain from making fun of your *Star Wars* remark. But don't worry. He just wants me to take a look at something."

She looked at him skeptically.

Stephen added, "Elon is too careful and smart to put a friend and long-retired CIA operative in danger."

She reluctantly replied, "It often seems like you're semi-retired on that front. But okay. Get back here quickly."

He leaned down, gave Jennifer a kiss, and said, "Deal. I'll be back ASAP." As he walked to the door, Stephen said, "Thanks for understanding, and I love you."

"Love you, too," Jennifer responded.

Stephen closed the door behind him.

After emerging from the Ian-Soho Hotel, it took Grant just over five minutes to walk to Mizrah's hotel. Grant was surprised that no one was at the desk in the lobby.

Well, it is three o'clock in the morning, I suppose.

At the same time, some unease grew inside Grant. As he entered the elevator, there was no way of knowing that, just a few minutes earlier, the desk clerk's body had been moved into the back office, and the security camera system had been shut down.

The elevator doors opened, and Grant exited onto the 14th floor. He began walking in the direction of the room number Mizrah had given him. With each step, Grant started to feel a growing tightness in his head. It had happened before. Grant took it as a signal that danger lurked. He called it a "red alert."

Before he could reach out to knock on the door, Grant heard sounds of glass shattering, bodies hitting the floor and a door banging from inside the room, all amidst grunting and curses being uttered.

Crap, and no weapon.

He lunged at the door knob, but it was locked. Grant took note that the doorframe was made of wood. He stepped back, raised his right leg in the air, and thrust it forward and down with all of the force he could muster. His foot hit the door just below the knob. The wood gave way, and the door swung open.

Grant took in the scene.

Closest was a man sitting on the floor, with his back against a wall and amidst shattered pieces of a wall mirror. He was trying to pull a long shard of glass from his stomach.

Farther into the room, another assailant, with his back to Grant, was sitting on top of Elon Mizrah. Grant could see Mizrah's hands releasing the man's shirt, and starting to fall to the carpet.

Beyond those two was a third attacker, who was positioned on his hands and knees, with his head hanging down.

When the door crashed open, Mizrah whispered, "Stephen..."

Each assailant turned in Grant's direction.

Grant immediately sprang forward.

The man on the floor stopped trying to remove the glass shard that Mizrah just seconds earlier had transformed into a weapon and plunged into his stomach. Grant landed on the man. With his right hand, he slammed the attacker's head to the floor, while at the same time, with his left, Grant finished the job of pulling the long piece of glass from the man's stomach. But Grant then plunged the shard into the man's neck.

When Grant entered, the man on top of Elon Mizrah had not moved, but did turn his head to see what was happening. Mizrah smiled weakly, and took in a deep breath. He looked down at the knife protruding just below his own chest. His attacker's grip on the handle had loosened. With his left hand, Mizrah ripped his opponent's hand off the knife, and then pulled the weapon out with his right hand. As the assaulter turned back, Mizrah raised the knife and returned the favor of plunging the knife into the attacker's chest.

As the man on top of Mizrah started to fall to the side, Grant was moving past his old friend to get to the third and final attacker. Grant noted the size of this last man, who had struggled to his feet. This assailant stood at six feet, seven inches – seven inches taller than Grant – and clearly spent most of his time in the gym. Grant saw, however, that he was still working to steady himself. The man was wavering, and had not yet raised the pistol that he had picked up off the carpet.

Elon must have hit you hard. Thankfully.

Grant drove his right shoulder into the man's stomach, wrapped his arms around him, and pushed forward. The two crashed through the hotel room's sliding glass door, and tumbled onto the balcony. Glass fell around them. The gun slipped from the assailant's hand, and his head struck the balcony's cement half-wall. This added to the man's disorientation, and maintained a slight advantage for Grant against the much larger, stronger and fitter opponent.

The attacker reached out with massive hands. Grant knew that if this person grabbed a hold of him, the fight would most likely be over, as Grant wouldn't have the strength to get free. Grant scrambled away, cutting his hands on the glass spread across the floor.

He quickly decided on a plan of action. Grant could move faster than his still off-balance opponent. He darted to his left. An opening materialized as the man tried to move to his feet. Grant slipped in back of him, jumped on his opponent's back, and wrapped his arms around the man's neck and tightened the hold with all of his strength. Grant had done this before, and knew it should take perhaps 15 or 20 seconds of cutting off the flow of oxygen for this attacker to pass out.

But things did not go as before.

The massive individual began to get up. Grant remained in place, trying to further tighten his grip.

His opponent actually managed to rise to his feet, with Grant still on his back, choking him.

No way. Come on.

The man started to reach up and around, flailing and striking at Grant, trying to grab him.

Despite the stranglehold on his neck, Grant could feel his opponent actually gaining strength.

How the hell?

Grant spotted the gun that had slid into the corner of the balcony, calculating that he would not have time to get to the weapon before being collected by this massive man.

His opponent pushed backwards, putting Grant at the edge of the balcony. He glanced down, seeing a car's headlights move by the hotel 14 floors down. Grant also noted the railing bar that ran around the top of the balcony's wall.

All or nothing. Dear Lord, help!

Grant swung his legs up and around his opponent's waist, using all of his remaining strength to squeeze and hopefully lock his legs in place. He then released his grip on the man's neck, and started to fall back. Grant grabbed hold of the balcony's bar. Using his own weight and pulling with his legs while his hands were locked onto the bar, Grant managed to pull the larger man up and started to bring him over the side of the balcony.

Surprise and probably some remaining wooziness worked against the assailant. He reached for Grant's head, but to no avail.

Grant swung him up and over the railing, and as his opponent was free of the balcony, Grant allowed his legs to go loose.

Grant felt the assailant's last attempt at survival, with a glance of a hand against the bottom of his jeans.

The attacker plunged face first down the 14 stories, and then crashed into the concrete sidewalk.

As his opponent began the descent to death, Grant had to somehow maintain his grip as the rest of his body swung around and crashed into the outside of the balcony. The force of his body hitting the balcony jarred his right hand loose. Grant hung precariously for a few seconds with his left hand positioned in the opposite direction necessary for having a reasonable shot at maintaining a grip. Pain jetted through his arm, into his shoulder and spread into his chest.

Lord, help.

Grant managed to pull his right hand back up, and grabbed hold of the railing. He flipped his left hand around, and pulled himself up and over the balcony wall. He fell to the floor, and was never so happy to receive further glass cuts on his hands and face.

Thank you, dear God.

He breathed in deeply.

Elon?

Grant jumped to his feet, and moved to his friend. Elon's eyes were barely open, and his breathing was shallow and labored. Upon seeing Grant, he whispered, "Glad to see you made it."

Grant replied, "Thanks to you. Stick with me, Elon."

Mizrah smiled faintly. "Too late." He tried to focus. "The laptop. Remember in Cairo..."

"What about Cairo? Elon."

Mizrah reached up and touched Grant's face with his fingertips. His hand slowly fell. His eyes closed, and then Elon Mizrah's breathing ceased.

Grant lowered his head and closed his eyes.

Dear Lord, I beg your forgiveness and mercy for Elon, and comfort for his family. His family...

Grant shook his head and sat back. He reached into his jeans pocket, and was surprised to find his phone undamaged. He found the name and hit the call.

"Stephen, what's going on?"

"Paige, it's not good. I need your help."

Chapter 14

The NYPD arrived first on the scene, but within a few minutes came a team of eight FBI special agents, accompanied by Paige Caldwell and Charlie Driessen. The FBI's quick arrival was thanks to orders from Supervisory Agent Rich Noack in Washington, D.C., after he had received a call from Caldwell. Driessen, Grant and Caldwell had a history – a combined colleagues-and-friends relationship – with Noack.

The FBI took over the scene, telling the NYPD that this was an engagement with terrorists, that the dead Israeli was with Mossad, and the name of the man who had stopped the terrorists, meaning Grant, could not be revealed to the public. FBI Special Agent John Smith added, "It's a matter of national security."

While the FBI did their work, including interviewing other hotel guests on the floor, searching their rooms, and then ordering those same people not to come out of those rooms, Caldwell and Driessen pulled Grant into an empty room down the hall.

Grant sat down in a chair. Caldwell pulled up a seat facing him, with a first-aid kit in hand. Driessen grabbed the edge of one of the beds.

Caldwell said, "I'm sorry about Mizrah."

Grant nodded slowly in response. He said, "Yeah, thanks." Grant was working to come down from the adrenaline high, and dealing with the loss of Elon. He offered no resistance as Caldwell took one of his hands and started cleaning his cuts.

Driessen looked at Grant and commented, "That was a hell of a mess. You're lucky to come out alive."

"I know."

As Caldwell continued to treat Grant's cuts on his hands and arms, the three once again reviewed the details of what had occurred – a process Grant already had gone through with the FBI.

Driessen added, "Well, there's no hiding a body that plummets 14 stories and splatters on a New York City sidewalk. But there are ways to control the how and why. It seems like the FBI has that covered."

Caldwell reached out for the cuts on Grant's face. But he leaned back, and said, "Thanks, Paige. I'm good."

We did this kind of thing a few times before, years ago, and we would have wound up in one of these beds.

Caldwell nodded, and said, "Right."

Get your head straight, Grant.

He stood up to start walking around the room.

Driessen asked, "So, Mizrah gave you no idea over the phone?"

Grant answered, "No. He just needed to show me something immediately. And before he died..." Grant paused and took a deep breath. "He said 'the laptop' and 'Remember in Cairo.' That was it."

Caldwell said, "So, what's the deal with Cairo?"

"That's where we met, and worked together." He looked directly at Caldwell. "It was just before you and I got together." He then continued walking around the room.

One of the few big things while at the CIA that I've avoided thinking about – a rare, successful attempt at compartmentalization.

Grant said, "Mossad and the CIA had their eyes on the same terrorist group. It turned out that an asset was working for both of us – for the CIA and for Mossad."

"How enterprising," commented Driessen.

"Yeah, but he never fed either one of us anything off base. He was committed, wanted to see Egypt and other parts of the Middle East and North Africa westernized, choose freedom over radicalism. He was smart, too; a rare and good man." Grant lowered his voice and head. "He had a big family as well."

Caldwell said, "Had?"

"His name was Amr Hegazy. He was supposed to meet both Elon and me one night. But he never showed. He simply disappeared."

"What happened?" asked Caldwell.

"Elon and I knew Amr didn't bail. Both of us, Mossad and CIA, did everything we could to find him, or at least find out what happened to him. We thought we were moving heaven and earth, but nothing. Then, about six months later, Elon received a package at his home. His wife had ordered some perishable food products. You know, being delivered in a Styrofoam cooler, packed in dry ice."

Caldwell and Driessen were silent.

Grant continued, "Thank God that it was Elon who opened it." He paused. "Amr's head was inside. Apparently, they intercepted the package, and made a statement."

Driessen merely whispered, "Shit."

Caldwell observed, "You never told me about this."

Grant replied, "Other than the Agency people involved, until right now, I never told anyone."

Not even Jen.

After nearly a minute of silence, Grant added, "Mossad tracked down and eliminated each person directly involved in Amr's death."

Caldwell observed, "Not surprising."

Driessen said, "So, assuming that the California assholes and these assholes were working together, the question now is: Are there any more of these particular assholes left, or was this it?"

Caldwell said, "In addition to what the FBI will be doing, we need to do our own homework." She turned to Grant.

"Sean is on his way into the city from Long Island. You need to give him everything when he gets here."

Grant nodded. "Of course."

"If anyone can figure out if others are involved, it's Sean." For Driessen and Grant, her observation was merely stating the obvious. Caldwell continued, "The FBI knows his skills as well, and they're giving Sean the first shot at Mizrah's computer and phone. Although, the phone seems like it was destroyed. But they didn't get to the laptop before you came along. Can you work with Sean on that as well?"

Grant nodded. "Give me a few minutes while I give Jen an update."

"Sure," replied Caldwell, and then she and Driessen left the room.

When Jennifer answered, Stephen could tell that she had not gone back to sleep. He began, "Listen, Jen, I'm okay."

She responded, "What happened?"

After Stephen finished relaying his encounter and what had happened to Elon Mizrah, Jen said in a low voice, "Dear God. Are you sure you're alright?"

"I am."

"I'm so sorry about Elon."

Stephen went on to talk briefly about Mizrah's family.

Eventually, Jennifer asked, "When will you be back here?"

"I'm actually not sure. Sean is on his way, and I not only have to give him a complete rundown on what happened and what I know, but I need to be here as he works to get into Elon's laptop."

"Okay. I understand."

Stephen knew the concern in her voice too well.

"Jen, I know you're going to want to push back on what I'm about to recommend."

"What is it?"

"I need you to head home."

"Without you? I don't think so."

"I know what you're thinking. But I'm going to have to help out on this whole mess now. And I'd be far less worried if I knew you were safe at home. I'd be better equipped to assist CDM and the FBI, to make sure nothing more happens."

Jennifer said, "Sometimes, Pastor Grant, you can be a pain in the ass."

Not the usual Jen. She's pissed.

"I know. I'm sorry, but..."

"Wait. No, I'm sorry for saying that. I understand that you're needed, you just saw your old friend die, more people's lives might be at risk, and you ... you almost..." Her voice broke.

"Jen, I really am sorry."

She breathed in deeply. "Stephen, I know. And so am I. I love you, and I can't help but worry."

He paused. "Jen, I love you, too, and if you want me..."

"Stop right there. Yes, I love you, and worry about you. But I certainly won't be the wife who stops you from helping people – whether in your role as pastor or as, well, whatever this is. We've talked about this before. It's just hard sometimes."

That's my Jen.

Jennifer continued, "I'll get ready to head home."

"Don't leave until I can get back to the room."

"Okay." Stephen heard her voice get back to normal. "But make no mistake, you owe me."

He smiled. "I get it."

"Big time. Like a few days in St. Louis to catch the Cardinals." Jennifer had been a Cardinals fan since childhood, while Stephen followed the Reds.

"That's a steep price, but sounds good."

After the call ended, Stephen opened the hotel room door, and signaled that Driessen and Caldwell could return. Caldwell was on the phone, but Driessen came back into the room.

"Is everything okay with Jennifer?" asked Driessen.

"As well as can be expected, given the circumstances."

"I've said it before, Grant. I don't get why she is with you. She's way too good for you."

"Yeah, I know, Charlie."

Caldwell came into the room.

Grant looked at his two friends and former CIA colleagues. "Any chance that Melissa would be willing to cancel or postpone the rest of the tournament?"

Caldwell smirked. "I called her while you were talking with Jennifer. She's open to it, but doesn't like the idea. I reviewed things with her, and she's going to listen to the assorted recommendations. But unless someone gives her something solid on a clear threat, and a direct, unequivocal recommendation to shut this down, I doubt it. I don't take her as the type to back down. But you know her better than I do."

Grant said, "You're right. She doesn't like the idea of giving up. I get it."

Caldwell confirmed, "So do I, and I'm with her."

And Driessen nodded his agreement.

Forty-five minutes later, Stephen waved as Jennifer pulled away in the Jeep. Ten minutes after that, he welcomed Sean McEnany into his room at the Ian-Soho.

While bringing his computer equipment through the door, McEnany said, "Let's make sure there are no more of these little shits lurking around."

Chapter 15

As Sean McEnany was getting set up in Grant's room, on another floor of the Ian-Soho, Ranya Khan answered a call from Prince Hkim Khan. Despite it being early this Saturday morning – just after 5:30 – she already was up.

"Father?"

"Yes, Ranya. Are you alright? Are you safe?"

"I am fine. What is wrong?"

Hkim answered, "There has been an incident, not far from you."

Ranya asked, "What does that mean?"

"I just heard that there was an altercation. Three men attacked and killed a Mossad agent in a hotel near yours."

"Really?"

"Yes, and the three, who were, unfortunately, Muslims from Egypt, were killed by one of the men working with CDM."

"I see," replied Ranya.

"Thankfully, the CDM people were there."

"You were wise to hire them."

"Ranya, you also need to know that others are part of the CDM group."

"I 'need to know.' Why?"

"Two of the players on the tour were inserted by CDM, in order to stay close to you."

"What? Who?"

"Jessica West and Brooke Semmler."

Ranya breathed deeply, but said nothing.

The prince continued, "Ranya, are you still there?"

"Yes, Father, I'm here. But you should have told me."

"I hired CDM to protect you, and they thought that this was important. They also didn't want you to treat their team any differently, or give anything away, even inadvertently."

Ranya again breathed in and out. She eventually said, "I see, Father. I still would have preferred to know. I am not some little girl who doesn't know what needs to be done."

Prince Khan apparently decided to ignore that last remark from his daughter. Instead, he said, "Yes, well, what about Anthony Deluca?"

"What about him?" The irritation in Ranya's voice grew.

"I was disappointed to hear that you broke up with him. He seemed like a good man, and I know his family."

"Father, just because you have done business with Tony's father does not mean that I want to continue dating the man."

"I understand, but..."

"No, Father, there are no 'buts.' This is what I've decided."

"Yes, I understand..."

Ranya cut her father off once again. "In addition, how did you find out about this? I assume it was from Hamza?"

"Of course, it was."

"And I assume that Hamza knew about West and Semmler being with CDM?"

"Yes, Ranya, he knew."

"You know, I'm starting to grow tired of this entire situation. Tired of Hamza being around me for years now, and the secrets regarding these CDM people."

"Shut up, Ranya."

"What?!"

"You heard me. Shut up. You 'grow tired'? Perhaps it is time for you to grow up. I am trying to do whatever I can to make things better in our nation, in this entire region. That has meant that my life, your life and the lives of everyone else in the family, everyone we care about, are at grave risk. And what are you doing? You are playing volleyball on the beach, complaining about people who are trying to keep you alive, and discarding a man who has cared for you and respected you for several years now."

Ranya took another deep breath, but it was uneven, with an underlying shakiness. Her face contorted. She finally said, "Perhaps I am doing more than you think."

He lashed out. "I doubt that."

Ranya rose from sitting on the edge of her bed, and began walking around the room – taking large strides. She unclenched a tight fist, and breathed in and out more smoothly now. She closed her eyes, stopped walking, and said, "I am sorry, Father. Forgive my selfishness and immaturity."

All traces of anger evaporated from Prince Hkim Khan's voice. "Of course, Ranya. And I am sorry for being so harsh."

They spoke a bit more about other family members, and before ending the call, Ranya said, "And Father, I will think more about Tony."

"Thank you, Ranya. Be safe."

"Good-bye, Father."

Ranya tossed her smart phone onto the bed, and looked at the door in the corner of the room. The key requirement that Hamza Alam had for each hotel they stayed in while on the Bedlam on the Beach tour was that Ranya's and his rooms would be adjacent, with an adjoining door. And Ranya was to keep it unlocked.

She knocked on the door, and then opened it.

Alam was seated at the hotel room desk with a laptop open. He looked over his shoulder at Ranya, and said with a trace of sarcasm, "Yes, please come in."

"I just spoke with my father."

"Good. How is the prince?"

"Apparently, you would know better than I."

Alam raised an eyebrow and crossed his arms. "You are somehow surprised that I speak to him regularly and keep him up-to-date, even given the reasons why I am assigned to be your security detail?"

Ranya sighed, and said, "No, I suppose I am not. But I do have a question."

"What is it?"

"Why didn't you tell me that West and Semmler worked for CDM?"

Alam simply replied, "What would have been the point?"

Ranya stared at him for a few seconds, and then she stepped back and closed the door between the two rooms. She also locked the door.

Chapter 16

The morning sunlight streamed into part of the room, splitting the wooden kitchen table down the middle between sunshine and shadow. The phone rested on the table in the light. Mostafa Ruhani sat next to the table, sipping a cup of coffee, in the shadow. The phone rumbled, moving slightly toward the relative darkness.

Ruhani looked at the phone. He put down the cup, and answered the call. "Yes?"

"Six dead and nothing to show for it."

Ruhani replied, "A dead Mossad agent is hardly nothing."

"So, it takes six of ours to kill one of theirs. I don't like that score," responded 11.

"Well, the key point is that he was stopped."

"No, you fool. He was not stopped. You did not acquire the information he had. It is in the hands of the enemy. It will not take long for them to put things together."

Ruhani sat up straighter, and anger rose in his voice. "I don't see how it is relevant for our purposes."

"Of course, you don't."

"Do not presume, you little shit. I have been fighting this war long before you entered the equation."

"That is quite true," said 11. "But it's time to start making a real difference."

"If you think we have not made a difference over the past quarter-century, you need to be reacquainted with what has been accomplished."

The tone in 11's voice shifted. "Fine. Are we still set to take the next step, even with losing the three?"

"I've made sure that it will work. Everything is fine."

"Good."

Ruhani warned, "Just make sure that you are set as well."

"Of course, I am."

The call was ended by 11. Ruhani put the phone down on the table, back in the sunlight.

Chapter 17

Ranya stepped out of the shower, and took one of the white towels off the rack. She watched in the mirror as she dried her skin and then her dark hair. She spun around, and then turned her head to look at her back in the reflective glass.

Ranya turned once again, continuing to gaze at herself. Her face didn't express satisfaction, disgust or anything in between. It showed nothing. She wrapped the towel around her, and walked out of the bathroom.

She picked up her phone, accessed her contacts, and placed a call to Anthony Deluca.

He answered, "What do you want?"

Her reply was soothing. "I want to apologize."

"And?"

"I've been thinking."

"Have you?"

"Tony, please don't make this more difficult. I've been thinking, and I think I made a mistake."

The anger and resentment in Deluca's voice began to dissipate. "Are you serious, Ranya?"

"I am."

A few seconds of silence passed.

Ranya said, "Are you still in the city?"

"Yes, I haven't left yet."

"Good. We need to talk."

Tony replied, "I'd like that."

"Well, here's my suggestion. Let's wait to have that discussion until this New York tournament is over. In the meantime, though, I'd really appreciate it if you might come to the event – at least to our matches."

"Um, sure, that's fine," replied Tony.

"Great," said Ranya.

A few seconds of awkward silence ended when Tony declared, "Ranya, I'll be there to root you and Melissa on. I'll see you later."

"Thanks, Tony."

Chapter 18

Grant was back at his courtside table for the first two side-by-side Saturday matches. However, Jennifer wasn't with him; nor was Elon Mizrah at the table across the court.

But a 10 mm Glock 20 kept Grant company. It was nestled in a holster in the small of his back, under a shirt and light jacket, and hidden from all others at this Bedlam on the Beach New York Open.

He also was in communication with allies, given that a tiny earpiece and smaller microphone kept him connected with Caldwell, Driessen, and Axelrod on the scene, as well as McEnany still sorting through information back in the hotel.

For good measure, the NYPD made a clear statement about its stepped-up presence, with a couple of patrol cars parked at the pier entrance, assorted uniformed officers sprinkled around the stands and court, and a harbor police boat moving in the waters of the Hudson River.

Even if some of this cell remains, they'd be crazy to try anything.

Then his thoughts turned to Elon dying hours earlier in front of his eyes, and his gaze moved to the Freedom Tower. His anger was stoked.

You know better. Assume nothing, Grant.

It didn't surprise Grant that Jessica West and Brooke Semmler lost their match in two sets. After what had happened during the overnight, the CDM duo were distracted from executing shots on the sand, instead, keeping watch on what was happening off the court.

During the second set of matches, Grant heard Sean McEnany's voice in his ear.

"Okay, listen up. I just linked to each of your phones. I think I've got something from Mizrah."

While West and Semmler were getting changed in the small women's locker room, Grant, Caldwell, Driessen and Axelrod, positioned at various points around the stadium, looked at their phones, clicking into the link set up by Sean.

Caldwell asked, "Everybody good?" After getting affirmative responses, she said, "Go ahead, Sean."

"Mizrah's phone basically is useless. But I was able to get into the laptop. Thankfully, he transferred assorted photos from his phone. I'm going to flip through these slowly as I'm talking. If anyone spots something, stop me." He started the process. "These pictures, you'll see, are focused on Ranya Khan. But he also has an assortment of crowd pictures. In fact, he has photos of each section of fans. From what I can tell, he was proceeding with scanning the faces for likely suspects."

Caldwell interrupted, "And did he find any?"

"Not sure yet." McEnany got back to the pictures. "Now, here, you'll see that he took individual pictures of seemingly everyone working or sitting courtside. By the way, he copied the photos of Stephen, Jennifer, Paige, Chase and Hamza Alam into a separate file."

Stephen commented, "Everyone courtside that he knew was security for Ranya, or at least somehow related to the effort."

Sean replied, "Right. Interestingly, though, only one person has a note attached. It's Alam, and Mizrah typed in, 'Amr'?"

Grant said, "What? He wrote 'Amr'?"

"Yes, what does it mean?"

"Crap."

It was Axelrod's turn to comment, "Who the hell is Amr?"

Grant didn't reply. He was now looking very closely at the picture of Hamza Alam.

Axelrod added, "Anyone?"

Driessen responded, "Hold on a minute, Chase."

Caldwell then said, "Stephen?"

Dear Lord, could it be?

Grant continued to look closely at the screen. "I can see it."

"What do you see?" asked McEnany.

Grant looked around to see if anyone was in earshot. But with the matches proceeding and music playing, the conversation was quite private. "Sean, I'll explain more fully later, but for now, I need you to work your magic and see if there's a potential link between a person who the CIA and Mossad worked with named Amr Hegazy and Hamza Alam." He gave McEnany the timeframe regarding Hegazy, as well as his ultimate fate. "Both Elon and I worked with Amr."

"What do you expect to find, Stephen?" asked Caldwell.

"Looking at this photo, my gut is telling me that Hamza Alam is one of the children of Amr Hegazy."

McEnany said, "I'm on it."

The call ended, and Grant said, "Yeah, so am I."

Driessen asked, "What does that mean?"

Grant queried, "Does anyone have a 20 on Alam?"

Axelrod, who was circulating in a club area at the top of the east stands, said, "Yes, he's positioned outside the locker rooms."

Grant replied, "Thanks." He got up and started to move toward the tunnel running under the west stands.

Caldwell asked, "What are you going to do?"

"I'm going to talk to Alam."

"And?"

"Time is not on our side. I'm going to be direct – find out if Amr was his father, and then I'm going to get a read on whether or not Alam really is on the side of the angels."

Driessen simply whispered, "Shit."

A new voice entered the conversation. "This is Jessica. Brooke and I just came out of the locker room. We can back up Stephen."

"Good. Thanks," said Caldwell.

Caldwell was again positioned with her back to the wall of the west stands. As Grant passed by, he looked in her blue eyes. He knew the look from years gone by. The message from Paige was: Get it done and be careful.

Grant's gaze turned upward into the stands. A severe face with intense, narrow eyes just a couple of rows up caught his brief attention. Grant didn't think anything of it, with his focus on Alam.

Chapter 19

Grant walked past the various booths and tents. As he approached Hamza Alam, West and Semmler hung back, watching from several yards away.

Alam tracked Grant as he drew closer, while glancing in the direction of West and Semmler as well.

Grant shut off his mic and earpiece, and stopped a few feet in front of Alam. He said, "Mr. Alam, my name is..."

Alam interrupted, "Stephen Grant. Yes, I know who you are."

Grant nodded, and then added, "What you probably are not aware of is that I knew your father."

Alam raised an eyebrow in response.

"Your father was Amr Hegazy, correct?"

Alam stared back at Grant for several seconds, and then responded, "What can I do for you, Pastor Grant?"

A few people were moving by the two men. Grant saw a spot away from the foot traffic. "Do you mind if we speak briefly over there?"

Alam nodded and accompanied Grant.

While away from the beach volleyball players and fans, Grant still spoke in a low voice. "I assume you are aware of the death of Elon Mizrah, as well as his three attackers."

Alam's response was silence.

Grant continued, "Elon and I both knew your father. He was a good man."

Alam shifted. Grant thought he looked a bit uncomfortable.

Alam finally replied, "And how did you two know my father?"

Grant briefly described Hegazy's work with Mossad and the CIA, as well as a reminder of the man's desire for a more open and westernized Middle East region. Grant added, "We did all we could in tracking down who murdered your father. In fact, our friends at Mossad, including Elon, made sure that those involved paid a heavy price."

Alam stared at the ground for nearly a minute. He looked up. Grant spotted moisture in his eyes that was not there previously. Alam extended his hand. "Thank you, Pastor Grant."

Grant shook Alam's hand, and said, "You know why I'm talking to you."

"Yes. I knew that Elon Mizrah was here and that he was Mossad. I also know that Israel is heartened by what Prince Khan is trying to do. Rest assured, Pastor Grant, that I am encouraged by the prince's efforts, and I know my father would have been as well. The prince also is aware of who my father was and his views. That's why I work for Prince Khan, and have been protecting his daughter for about five years now."

Grant said, "I understand. Thank you. And by the way, before leaving New York, if you would like to sit down for a conversation, I think you'd appreciate some of the things I could tell you about your father."

"Yes, I'd like that. For now, I need to get back to work."

"Yeah, so do I."

"A second job, in addition to St. Mary's?"

Grant smiled, and said, "That's not the intention, but it sometimes seems so."

As he turned to head back to his courtside seat, Grant nodded at West and Semmler. The duo moved to their next assignment, which was circulating among the booths and tents set up outside the stadium.

Grant re-opened communications with the CDM group. He announced, "Alam is good."

Before entering the tunnel under the stands, Grant looked over at the Bedlam on the Beach booth. Maggie Stone was running things, with Tom in the back ready to provide whatever help his wife might need. Stephen nodded at Tom, who returned the action. Grant then moved into the tunnel.

On the sand, next to the men's match, Melissa Ambler and Ranya Khan began their contest. While watching from his seat in the stands, Mostafa Ruhani whispered into his own small microphone, "It has started."

One row over from Ruhani sat Tony Deluca.

Several miles east of the Bedlam on the Beach tournament, three men in a small warehouse in Brooklyn mounted and started up motorcycles.

West of the beach volleyball event, two kayaks slipped from a large white yacht into the waters of the Hudson River. The two kayakers wearing backpacks immediately started paddling toward the music, fans and volleyball competitors.

Another small, fast boat lurked not too far off in the distance.

Chapter 20

As Grant sat back down at his table, Caldwell moved to the other side of the court. She now positioned her back against the wall of the east stands.

Axelrod maintained his position in the club, from which he could look down on the booths outside the stadium, on the court and stands, and parts of the surrounding water. And Driessen stood in the top row of the west stands, with a clear look all around the Hudson and his own angle on the stands and court.

Sean McEnany's voice returned in the ears of Grant and the rest of the CDM team. "Okay. This is important. I've identified one of the faces in the crowd from a couple of Mizrah's photos, and it's not good. He's an old, elusive hand in the business of Islamic terrorism, and has gone by assorted names over the years, but his real name is Mostafa Ruhani. You have access to a few pics of him. I'm also sending these to the FBI and NYPD." McEnany paused, then added, "And Stephen, a source in Europe told me that Mossad missed one target in the Amr Hegazy killing."

"Ruhani?"

"That's the word."

*　　*　　*

As they were speaking, the NYPD patrol boat slowly turned in the narrow area between Piers 26 and 25. The boat was only 15 to 20 yards behind Grant.

* * *

On the court, Ranya Khan had the ball in her hands, and was walking back to the service zone. She and Melissa Ambler had just won a point – to the delight of many of the fans. The event DJ turned the music up. John Mellencamp's "Authority Song" began streaming forth from the massive speakers.

* * *

Caldwell replied, "Thanks, Sean."
Grant pulled up the photos, and whispered, "Shit."

* * *

*"They like to get you in a compromising position.
They like to get you there and smile in your face.
They think, they're so cute when they got you in
that condition. Well I think, it's a total disgrace."*

* * *

One of the kayakers approached the patrol boat. The man paddling smiled, waved and called out to the police, "Excuse me! I'm sorry, but I'm hurt."
An officer came closer to the edge of the boat, and waved the kayaker over. "What's the matter?"

* * *

McEnany said, "What is it?"
Grant answered, "I saw this guy."
Caldwell asked, "Where?"

* * *

"I fight authority, authority always wins. I been doing it, since I was a young kid. I've come out grinnin'. I fight authority, authority always wins."

*   *   *

The kayaker replied, "Hold on. I'll show you."

From the top row, the interaction on the water caught the attention of Driessen. He watched.

The man in the kayak reached into his backpack, and flipped a switch on a detonator attached to a package of C4. The terrorist then tossed the backpack up onto the deck of the boat.

The officer said, "What the hell?"

*   *   *

"So I call up my preacher. I say: 'Gimme strength for Round 5.' He said: 'You don't need no strength, you need to grow up, son.' I said: 'Growing up leads to growing old and then to dying, and dying to me don't sound like all that much fun.'"

*   *   *

Grant stood up, and said, "He was just a couple of..."

The force of the blast ripped into the patrol boat. The four officers on board were instantaneously killed, with parts of their bodies scattered into the air and water.

Among the fans sitting at other tables along the south side of the court, though badly hurt, most were still breathing.

Given that he was standing, the blast tossed Grant forward. His body somersaulted in the air, and his back hit the sand on the volleyball court.

*   *   *

The men's and women's teams, and officials on the courts, were knocked off their feet. Minor injuries were the rule, along with being dazed and confused.

The one person on the sand clearly not confused, though, was Ranya Khan. She moved into a crouched position, with her eyes darting around.

*   *   *

The explosion shook both stands. Driessen grabbed the railing to steady himself. "Holy shit."

He pulled his focus away from the site of the explosion, and turned to look at the water.

Driessen pulled a Glock 21 out from under his shirt, and looked directly down to see another kayaker paddling up to the edge of the pier. The person started to pull a backpack off his shoulders.

Driessen mumbled, "No way, you little shit."

He leaned over the railing to get a better view, aimed his gun, and fired off three shots. Two hit the target with one projectile entering the terrorist's shoulder and the other penetrating the side of his skull. The man's head rocked and then fell back lifeless.

The backpack rolled off the kayak into the water, where it began to drift and sink.

Driessen announced into his microphone, "One down."

*   *   *

"Oh no. Oh no. I fight authority, authority always wins."

*   *   *

With the explosion, half of the police officers guarding the entrance to the pier turned and headed in the direction of the blast. The others remained, with weapons drawn, alert for attacks coming from another direction. That attack came in just a few seconds.

Three black motorcycles shot out of North Moore Street, and across West Street. Each rider reached over his head and pulled out an Uzi submachine gun, and started firing at the police officers. The NYPD returned fire, but two fell with gunshot wounds. The riders sped around barriers and by the patrol cars, and began the turn onto the pier.

One police officer calmly tracked the last rider, and fired off several shots. The rider was hit. As the bike began to slide, his body went head first into one of the cement barriers.

The two remaining motorcycle attackers raced forward, and fired into people both inside and outside the various booths.

In the Bedlam on the Beach booth, Father Tom Stone scanned the area. He then grabbed Maggie and her assistant by the arms. He said, "Move this way." He directed the two to the back of the booth, and all three took cover behind stacked cases of Bedlam on the Beach merchandise.

Out in the open, Jessica West announced, "I have the guy on the right."

Brooke Semmler replied, "Got it."

West hit her target with the first two shots. The rider tumbled off the bike and onto the ground, sliding under one of the tents. As people ran and screamed around her, West rushed toward the felled attacker. The terrorist was moaning and moving slightly. West raised her gun, and fired two shots through the shield of the motorcycle helmet and into the man's face.

West reported, "Another down."

*   *   *

While West was firing at the attacker on the right, Semmler was doing the same at her target. But her four shots missed their mark. One of the return salvos from the terrorist caught her right shoulder. As Semmler was thrown off balance, the rider continued to race forward. When he came upon her, he stuck out his boot, and landed a blow to Semmler's hip that sent her spinning and crashing to the ground.

From the top of the stands, Chase Axelrod was waiting for a clear shot.

As the rider moved past Semmler, everyone left among the booths was moving away from the death being spewed from the motorcycle.

With his Glock 20 trained, he whispered to himself, "Now."

Axelrod unleashed a succession of six shots. Three plunged through the assailant's backpack. The man fell forward, but somehow stayed on the bike and the motorcycle itself remained upright and moving. It turned to the right, and went head on into a concrete barrier. The terrorist was launched forward. Death arrived when his body slammed into the water.

*   *   *

Right after the blast went off, Mostafa Ruhani moved quickly. He jumped over the front railing, landed on the sand, and rolled. He stood up, and moved toward Ranya Khan.

Hamza Alam, who had been knocked down by the explosion, was just a few feet away, and began to get to his feet. Ruhani took a gun out and pointed it at Alam, who stopped moving. Ruhani called out, "You are an infidel just like your father was." He pulled the trigger, and Alam fell to the sand.

Across the courts, Paige Caldwell had just watched Grant get launched by the blast, and land on the sand.

Ruhani turned and began running at Khan, who was on the north side of the court next to Melissa Ambler. Caldwell was moving toward Grant who was sprawled out on the south side of the same court. Both Ruhani and Caldwell had a gun in hand.

Khan watched unmoving as Ruhani approached.

A few feet away, Ambler was lying on the sand, and managed to push herself up onto her elbows. With the gun in his right hand, Ruhani reached out with his left to Khan. He said, "Eleven, we need to go now."

Gunshots could be heard from the west and east sides of the stadium.

Khan spat her response at Ruhani. "This is it, you fool? You've botched it."

"Eleven, forgive me."

Ambler was looking up at the two and listening to the exchange. She said, "Ranya, what the hell is going on? Who is this and why is he calling you 'Eleven'?"

Ruhani urged, "The boat is arriving to get us across the river while things are still in chaos."

Khan looked at Ambler with disgust, and standing in her yellow bikini, she declared, "He calls me 'Eleven' out of respect. I chose it to remind everyone of Muhammed's eleven wives, and that they, too, served Allah in ways that you Western infidels cannot fathom." She turned to Ruhani, "Quickly, give me your gun."

* * *

Tony Deluca went untouched by the explosion. He momentarily, though, stood in shock at what was going on around him. And then he watched a man gun down Hamza Alam right in front of him.

Deluca moved, climbing over the front railing of the stands, falling to the ground, and made his way to Alam.

* * *

Caldwell fell at Grant's side in the sand. "Stephen! Are you alright?"

Grant groaned. "Crap. My head is spinning." He sucked air in deeply, and pushed himself up to a sitting position. Looking over Caldwell's shoulder, he spotted Ruhani. "Paige, Ruhani." He raised his arm with some effort and pointed.

Caldwell turned, sprang to her feet, and began running toward Ruhani, who was standing in front of Ranya Khan and over Melissa Ambler. Caldwell slowed slightly, moving under the volleyball net. Ruhani handed his gun to Khan, but that didn't divert Caldwell from her objective. Neither Khan nor Ruhani saw Caldwell coming. She drove her shoulder into Ruhani's side, and landed on top of him in the sand. But Ruhani managed to roll, and maneuvered himself on top of Caldwell.

At the same time, Ambler tried to act. She moved to her feet and toward Khan. But she was met with a sweep of Khan's gun to the side of her head. Ambler fell to the sand.

By this point, Grant had managed to get to his knees and draw his gun.

Ruhani, meanwhile, had maneuvered so that he could wrap his hands around Caldwell's neck. Rather than trying to fight off his clutch, Caldwell struggled to reposition her Glock. But as Ruhani's grip tightened, the gun slipped from her hand. Caldwell grabbed Ruhani's arms, and pulled. He was too strong.

Caldwell was looking up and saw Ruhani's forehead lurch violently backwards. Blood splattered, with drops falling on her face.

Caldwell was able to stretch her head back to see Hamza Alam standing with a gun in his hand, while his shirt was red with blood. Behind him stood Anthony Deluca.

As Ruhani fell to the side, Khan had just struck Ambler, and now she turned the gun on Alam. She saw Deluca as well, and yelled, "Both of you!"

At the same time, Deluca and Alam each said, "Ranya?"

She proclaimed, "I am so sick of you two."

Grant struggled to focus his vision.

God, please.

Clarity came and he fired off two shots. Both hit home. The first entered between Ranya Khan's shoulder blades, and the second ripped into the middle of her back and through her spine.

Grant's vision went cloudy once more, and he fell forward onto the sand.

The music had played on throughout the bedlam, and now the song came to its close.

"I fight authority, authority always wins."

Chapter 21

The second kayaker who was shot by Charlie Driessen had an even larger package of C4. If it had been detonated, it likely would have brought down the west side stands.

Similarly, in addition to the submachine guns, the three motorcyclists had explosives meant for the east stands and the pier.

In the hours after the attack, an FBI manhunt was under way for the three members of the terrorist group still missing – two at the helm of the yacht and the other guiding the smaller boat that was supposed to serve as the escape vehicle for Mostafa Ruhani, Ranya Khan, or Eleven, and any of the motorcycle riders or kayakers who survived. It turned out that none of them did survive – despite heroic efforts by emergency personnel. The death count for the victims came to seventeen, including the four officers on the patrol boat.

The coming days and weeks would reveal the links between Ruhani and Ranya Khan. It had started halfway through her college years. There already was anger and resentment brewing in Ranya Khan, so it didn't take much work for Ruhani to radicalize her, and have her turn against Prince Khan and his efforts. Later, Ruhani loved Ranya's idea for joining the beach volleyball circuit in order to use it as a target of "American decadence," and then having her take credit for the attacks and publicly denounce her father. Ranya and Ruhani had assumed the prince would be weakened by his daughter and the attacks – about that, they would be proven correct.

Hamza Alam was a perceptive security operative, but Ranya turned out to be his blind spot. He would come to realize that much should have been obvious when it came to Ranya's radicalization and rise to become the mysterious Eleven. Yet, he simply was never able, or willing, to see it. He would confess to a broken-hearted Prince Khan, "Ranya came to feel like a daughter to me as well."

Hours after the attack, the FBI gave a ride home to Stephen Grant, Tom and Maggie Stone, and Melissa Ambler. While Tom and Maggie came out of the day's conflict without physical injuries, Melissa was nursing a swollen cheek, and Stephen shifted carefully in the SUV's seat given his various cuts, abrasions, deep bruises, and misaligned spine, along with a concussion.

Rather than going to her house in Quogue, Melissa took Tom and Maggie up on their invitation to stay at their place.

From the SUV, Grant watched Tom, Maggie and Mel walk toward the front door of the Stone home.

This is going to be tough on Melissa, and she's already been through so much with losing Mike. Lord, please be with her, give her strength, and help her find peace in You.

Ten minutes later, the FBI Suburban stopped on the circular driveway of the Grant home.

Grant looked at the person who was driving. "Thank you, Special Agent Smith, for your help."

"You're welcome, and thanks for what you've done, Pastor Grant. And not just for today. Agents Noack and Nguyen speak highly of you, and I'm familiar with your role in assorted, let's say, other events in recent times."

Grant replied, "I'm often surprised at the situations I sometimes find myself in."

"Well, it does seem pretty weird for a pastor, but I'm glad you do find yourself in those situations. You help and protect people."

The front door of the house opened, and out came Jennifer.

The two men shook hands, and Grant said, "God bless you, Agent Smith."

"And you, Pastor Grant. By the way, if you think of it, keep me in your prayers."

"You got it."

Jen opened the SUV door, and Stephen carefully eased himself out of the vehicle.

Jen said, "Thank God you're home."

Stephen put his arm around his wife's shoulder, and Jennifer carefully slipped her arm around his back.

As the SUV pulled away and moved down the driveway, Stephen leaned on Jennifer, as she guided him into their home.

Chapter 22

After the early Sunday service at St. Bartholomew's Anglican Church, Melissa Ambler returned to the Stone home. She sat alone in the yard, looking out at the small lake where the back lawn of the church and rectory ended.

Just after noon, Father Tom Stone joined her, claiming the lawn chair next to Melissa's. He asked, "How are you?"

"I have no idea. I feel lost. I'm doubting myself."

"Hey, I'm here to listen."

Melissa smiled. "Thanks. I don't know where to start. I have so much pinging around my brain. Why did I let the tournament continue?"

"From what I understand, that's the advice you received from everyone involved, including all of the law enforcement and security experts."

She nodded, and added, "Yes. But I could have simply cancelled it."

"I understand the feeling of regret, but none of this is your fault in any way. We know who bears responsibility."

The two sat quietly for a couple of minutes. Melissa then said, "It helped going to church this morning."

"I'm glad."

"But it's been hard to go to church without Mike."

"Why?"

Melissa declared, "Our faith was our foundation. And oddly, since it wasn't popular to note our faith in either of our work worlds, that only brought us closer together."

Tom said, "I understand."

"So, whenever I went to church, I would think about Mike in a different way than I do at Corevana or even at home. And ... well ... I got sad. I know that's not right, not what I should be..." Tears began streaming from her eyes and sliding down her cheeks.

Tom replied, "It's not wrong, Melissa. I understand, and the Lord certainly does."

She asked, "Do you think so?"

He smiled in response. "Yeah, I do."

Melissa wiped away her tears. "Even with everything I've been doing, I still feel unsure and adrift without Mike and without being at church."

"You're not alone. Jesus spoke about building your house on rock or on the sand. He is the rock. Our faith in Him is the rock. Without that, it's shifting sands." He paused, and added, "And I'm not talking beach volleyball sand."

Melissa smiled. "So, what do I do?"

Tom looked out at the lake. "Ah, the big question. I have no great insights. Take the time to heal, and to pray. It helps me to try to make a conscious effort to inject a few moments of prayer into the day. I call them on-the-run prayers – just some silent praying while driving or doing whatever. It helps to keep things in perspective."

Melissa simply replied, "Okay."

Tom added, "As for church, you're part of the St. Bart's family, and I assume part of the family at the parish you and Mike attended in California as well."

She volunteered, "St. George's."

Tom looked Melissa directly in the eyes, and said, "Coming to the church that you and Mike shared shouldn't be a moment of sadness, but rather a place of joy, peace and comfort. It should serve as a tangible reminder of the hope that we have in Jesus and what He's done for each of us – taking on our sin, conquering death and offering redemption and salvation. Without the rock, this life can be perplexing, unsteady and difficult."

Liquid started to accumulate in Melissa's eyes once again. Barely above a whisper, she said, "I know that's how it should be..."

Tom said, "We'll take each step together. Maggie and I are here for you, of course, as is St. Bart's."

Melissa said, "Thanks, Tom. And I have to tell Maggie thanks as well. I love you guys."

Tom replied, "And we love you."

Chapter 23

Pastor Stephen Grant, largely against the wishes of Jennifer, made it to St. Mary's Lutheran Church for the two Divine Services on Sunday morning. He played assistant to Pastor Zack Charmichael.

After each service, the parishioners, who knew or found out that Grant had been at the beach volleyball tournament that was attacked the previous day, expressed thanks to God for his being safe, and asked about what had happened and how he felt. They didn't know his role in the events.

After everyone else had left the church, Zack and his wife, Cara, invited Jennifer and Stephen to their house. Zack said, "Why don't you guys come over? You can relax and decompress."

Stephen responded, "Thanks. It's much appreciated, but do you mind if we take a rain check? I need to get some actual bed rest, I think."

Jennifer interrupted, "Yes, you do."

Zack smiled, and said, "No worries."

Cara added, "I'm so glad that you're okay, Stephen."

"Me, too," said Zack. "By the way, you're not going to get away with just saying that you were at the tournament. Tom and Maggie provided some additional information, and I want the entire story."

Cara was Tom and Maggie's daughter, and therefore, they were Zack's in-laws.

Stephen replied, "Yes, well, let's keep that on the QT."

Less than a half hour later, Jennifer was getting behind the wheel of the Jeep, with Stephen settling in next to her in the passenger seat.

He groaned slightly, and said, "This didn't used to hurt this much."

"You've been blown up before?"

"Well..."

Jennifer interrupted, "Of course, you have."

As she steered the vehicle down the church's driveway, Stephen said, "Jen, thanks for everything."

She looked over at her husband, and smiled. "Hey, I love you, no matter how much trouble you are."

Stephen chuckled.

Jennifer turned the Jeep onto the road. She then added, "Seriously, thank you. I know that you're behind me in everything I do, and I hope I'm doing the same for you."

"You most certainly are."

"I've come to fully appreciate what you do," observed Jennifer.

"What do you mean?"

Jennifer answered, "You play important and very different roles in helping to save people. You do this thing now and then linked to your old career where you save and protect people physically. And then there's Pastor Grant who brings the Good News to people through Word and sacrament. That's the ultimate help." She paused and then commented, "I've always appreciated all of this – my two Stephen Grants – but you know how you get one of those clarifying moments or reminders in life now and then?"

"I sure do."

"That happened to me yesterday, while I was driving home and then waiting to hear that you were alright amidst the chaos."

Stephen repeated what he said just moments earlier. "Thanks."

A few minutes later, Jennifer turned the Jeep down their street. "Now, we're going to get you into bed, so you can get better. And maybe later in the week, you'll be able to do more in bed than just sleep it off."

"Sounds good. You can count on it."

Jennifer smiled, and said, "We'll see. After all, it hurts more and takes longer to bounce back from explosions because you're older now."

"Okay, I'm not thanking you for that one."

They exited the Jeep, and Jennifer gave him some support as they walked to the door of the house.

"No argument, correct? Straight into bed?"

Stephen answered, "Just two things."

"Stephen?" replied Jennifer with exasperation.

He said, "Just two calls, and I can make them from bed. I have to check on Hamza Alam, and if he's up to it, tell him more about his father. And then I need to speak with Elon's wife."

Jennifer nodded. "Of course." She reached up, pulled her husband's head a bit closer, and kissed his cheek. "I love you," she declared.

Chapter 24

Two weeks later

The first three days of the "Bedlam on the Beach in Boston" tournament had been a wild success. Support came from across the nation and around the world.

The stadium had been erected alongside the Charles River, and attendance was overflowing.

For good measure, on Sunday afternoon, the women's tournament was staring at a potential fairy tale ending.

With Brooke Semmler on the mend from the injuries suffered in New York, Jessica West and Melissa Ambler teamed up for the season's final event. And here they were playing a third set against Kelsey Gale and Sunny Sackett.

The men's final on the adjacent court had ended in two sets, so the crowd's attention was fully on the West/Ambler vs. Gale/Sackett contest.

In the stands were Tom and Maggie Stone. Their nervousness was evident throughout the match.

Meanwhile, each person from CDM International Strategies and Security was in attendance as well. In fact, CDM had two of the courtside tables. Caldwell, Driessen, McEnany and Axelrod were at one, while Kent Holtwick, Brooke and Phil Lucena sat around the other.

Phil and Brooke were the most invested, for obvious reasons, in the match, with each silently, and at times not so silently, urging Jessica, and her partner, forward. While also watching the points going back and forth on the court, Kent doted on Brooke, making sure she was comfortable.

On the court, Sackett provided a perfect set for Gale, who jumped in the air, and struck the ball that eluded Ambler's block. But West managed a full extension dig, and kept the point going. The ball, however, sailed in the wrong direction. Somehow, though, Ambler caught up with its descent at the back of the court. She managed to launch the ball back toward the net. The knowledgeable fans in the stands could see that West was completely out of position, and the ball was not going to cross over the net. Ambler's attempt also lacked the height needed for West to recover. At least, that's how it seemed.

With her back to the net, West backpedaled, glanced over her shoulder at the opponents, looked up at the ball, and then leaped high into the air. With her back still to the net, she swung her right hand into the air, and attempted a blind spike over her shoulder.

It wasn't the speed of the shot, but instead its placement. Sackett was positioned a bit too close to the center, leaving space on the side. That's where West's shot was headed. Sackett dove, but it wasn't enough. The ball landed on the line.

The crowd exploded in appreciation.

Both Phil and Brooke sprang to their feet, as if they were completely healed.

Ambler gave West a high five and a hug. She said, "Amazing. Now, let's end this."

No one sat down as West was about to serve match point. She slowly walked toward the service zone, spotted Phil and Brooke, and smiled at both.

Brooke leaned over, and said to Phil, "She really is an outstanding player."

"I know," he responded.

"Is she actually considering a move to try this fulltime?"

Phil looked at Brooke, and replied, "She loves this, and she loves CDM. So, I have no idea what she's going to do, and neither does she, at this point."

West surprised everyone by sending a soft serve down the middle of the court. Wonder grew among all in attendance. Would the ball land inside or beyond the end line? Gale and Sackett seemed to agree that it was heading out of bounds, and let it fly by. They were wrong. The ball hit the sand inside the end line.

The crowd erupted.

Phil, Brooke and Kent formed a group hug, while jumping up and down.

Gale and Sackett's shoulders sagged.

Ambler and West screamed in victory, hugged each other, and fell to the sand.

The beach volleyball fairy tale had come true.

Acknowledgments

Thank you to the members of the Pastor Stephen Grant Fellowship for their support:

Ultimate Readers
Jody Baran

Bronze Readers
Michelle Behl
Tyrel Bramwell
Gregory Brown
Mike Eagle
Sue Kreft

Readers
Robert Rosenberg

As always, thanks to Beth for her love, edits and insights. I also thank my two sons, David and Jonathan. They inspire me, and I appreciate their senses of humor.

Thanks to The Reverend Tyrel Bramwell for creating the cover for this book. Once again, shortcomings in my books are always all about me, and no one else.

I appreciate that so many friends and fans have found some enjoyment in reading my books. And I thank all of them for the encouragement.

As long as someone keeps reading, I'll keep writing. God bless.

Ray Keating
October 2018

About the Author

This is Ray Keating's second Pastor Stephen Grant short story, and the tenth entry in the overall Pastor Stephen Grant series. The first eight novels are *Warrior Monk*, followed by *Root of All Evil?*, *An Advent for Religious Liberty*, *The River*, *Murderer's Row*, *Wine Into Water*, *Lionhearts*, and *Reagan Country*, along with the short story *Heroes and Villains*.

Keating also is an author of various nonfiction books, an economist, and a podcaster. His latest nonfiction book is *The Realistic Optimist TO DO List & Calendar 2019*. In addition, he is the editor/publisher/columnist for DisneyBizJournal.com. Keating was a columnist with RealClearMarkets.com, and a former weekly columnist for *Newsday*, *Long Island Business News*, and the *New York City Tribune*. His work has appeared in a wide range of additional periodicals, including *The New York Times*, *The Wall Street Journal*, *The Washington Post*, *New York Post*, Los Angeles *Daily News*, *The Boston Globe*, *National Review*, *The Washington Times*, *Investor's Business Daily*, New York *Daily News*, *Detroit Free Press*, *Chicago Tribune*, *Providence Journal Bulletin*, *TheHill.com*, *Touchstone* magazine, *Townhall.com*, *Newsmax*, and *Cincinnati Enquirer*. Keating lives on Long Island with his family.

Enjoy All of the Pastor Stephen Grant Adventures!

Paperbacks and Kindle versions at Amazon.com

Signed books at raykeatingonline.com

• *Heroes and Villains: A Pastor Stephen Grant Short Story* by Ray Keating

As a onetime Navy SEAL, a former CIA operative and a pastor, many people call Stephen Grant a hero. At various times over the years defending the Christian Church and the United States, he has journeyed across the nation and around the world. But now Grant finds himself in an entirely unfamiliar setting – a comic book, science fiction and fantasy convention. But he still joins forces with a unique set of heroes in an attempt to foil a villainous plot against one of the all-time great comic book writers and artists.

• *Reagan Country: A Pastor Stephen Grant Novel* by Ray Keating

Could President Ronald Reagan's influence reach into the former "evil empire"? The media refers to a businessman on the rise as "Russia's Reagan." Unfortunately, others seek a return to the old ways, longing for Russia's former "greatness." The dispute becomes deadly. Conflict stretches from the Reagan Presidential Library in California to the White House to a Russian Orthodox monastery to the Kremlin. Stephen Grant, pastor at St. Mary's Lutheran Church on Long Island, a former Navy SEAL and onetime CIA operative, stands at the center of the tumult.

• *Lionhearts: A Pastor Stephen Grant Novel* by Ray Keating

War has arrived on American soil, with Islamic terrorists using new tactics. Few are safe, including Christians, politicians, and the media. Pastor Stephen Grant taps into his past with the Navy SEALS and the CIA to help wage a war of flesh and blood, ideas, history, and beliefs. This is about defending both the U.S. and Christianity.

• *Wine Into Water: A Pastor Stephen Grant Novel* by Ray Keating

Blood, wine, sin, justice and forgiveness... Who knew the wine business could be so sordid and violent? That's what happens when it's infiltrated by counterfeiters. A pastor, once a Navy SEAL and CIA operative, is pulled into action to help unravel a mystery involving fake wine, murder and revenge. Stephen Grant is called to take on evil, while staying rooted in his life as a pastor.

• *Murderer's Row: A Pastor Stephen Grant Novel* by Ray Keating

How do rescuing a Christian family from the clutches of Islamic terrorists, minor league baseball in New York, a string of grisly murders, sordid politics, and a pastor, who once was a Navy SEAL and CIA operative, tie together?

Murderer's Row is the fifth Pastor Stephen Grant novel, and Keating serves up fascinating characters, gripping adventure, and a tangled murder mystery, along with faith, politics, humor, and, yes, baseball.

• *The River: A Pastor Stephen Grant Novel* by **Ray Keating**

Some refer to Las Vegas as Sin City. But the sins being committed in *The River* are not what one might typically expect. Rather, it's about murder. Stephen Grant once used lethal skills for the Navy SEALs and the CIA. Now, years later, he's a pastor. How does this man of action and faith react when his wife is kidnapped, a deep mystery must be untangled, and both allies and suspects from his CIA days arrive on the scene? How far can Grant go – or will he go – to save the woman he loves? Will he seek justice or revenge, and can he tell the difference any longer?

• *An Advent for Religious Liberty: A Pastor Stephen Grant Novel* by **Ray Keating**

Advent and Christmas approach. It's supposed to be a special season for Christians. But it's different this time in New York City. Religious liberty is under assault. The Catholic Church has been called a "hate group." And it's the newly elected mayor of New York City who has set off this religious and political firestorm. Some people react with prayer – others with violence and murder. Stephen Grant, former CIA operative turned pastor, faces deadly challenges during what becomes known as "An Advent for Religious Liberty." Grant works with the cardinal who leads the Archdiocese of New York, the FBI, current friends, and former CIA colleagues to fight for religious liberty, and against dangers both spiritual and physical.

• *Root of All Evil? A Pastor Stephen Grant Novel* by Ray Keating

Do God, politics and money mix? In *Root of All Evil?*, the combination can turn out quite deadly. Keating introduced readers to Stephen Grant, a former CIA operative and current parish pastor, in the fun and highly praised *Warrior Monk*. Now, Grant is back in *Root of All Evil?* It's a breathtaking thriller involving drug traffickers, politicians, the CIA and FBI, a shadowy foreign regime, the Church, and money. Charity, envy and greed are on display. Throughout, action runs high.

• *Warrior Monk: A Pastor Stephen Grant Novel* by Ray Keating

Warrior Monk revolves around a former CIA assassin, Stephen Grant, who has lived a far different, relatively quiet life as a parish pastor in recent years. However, a shooting at his church, a historic papal proposal, and threats to the pope's life mean that Grant's former and current lives collide. Grant must tap the varied skills learned as a government agent, a theologian and a pastor not only to protect the pope, but also to feel his way through a minefield of personal challenges.

All of the Pastor Stephen Grant novels are available at Amazon.com and signed books at www.raykeatingonline.com.

Join the Pastor Stephen Grant Fellowship!

Visit
www.patreon.com/pastorstephengrantfellowship

Consider joining the Pastor Stephen Grant Fellowship to enjoy more of Pastor Stephen Grant and the related novels, receive new short stories, enjoy special thanks, gain access to even more content, receive special gifts, and perhaps even have a character named after you, a friend or a loved one.

Ray Keating declares, "I've always said that I'll keep writing as long as someone wants to read what I write. Thanks to reader support from this Patreon effort, I will be able to pen more Pastor Stephen Grant and related novels, while also generating short stories, reader guides, and other fun material. At various levels of support, you can become an essential part of making this happen, while getting to read everything that is written before the rest of the world, and earning other exclusive benefits – some that are pretty darn cool!"

Readers can join at various levels...

• **Reader Level at $4.99 per month...**

You receive all new novels FREE and earlier than the rest of the world, and you get FREE exclusive, early reads of new Pastor Stephen Grant short stories throughout the year. In addition, your name is included in a special "Thank You" section in forthcoming novels, and you gain access to the private Pastor Stephen Grant Fellowship Facebook page, which includes daily journal entries from Pastor Stephen Grant, insights from other characters, regular recipes from Grillin' with the Monks, periodic videos and Q&A's with Ray Keating, and more!

- **Bronze Reader Level at $9.99 per month...**

All the benefits from the above level, plus you receive two special gift boxes throughout the year with fun and exclusive Pastor Stephen Grant merchandise.

- **Silver Reader Level at $22.99 per month...**

All the benefits from the above levels, plus you receive two additional (for a total of four) special gift boxes throughout the year with fun and exclusive Pastor Stephen Grant merchandise, and you get a signed, personalized (signed to you or the person of your choice as a gift) Pastor Stephen Grant novel three times a year.

- **Gold Reader Level at $39.99 per month...**

All the benefits from the above levels, plus your name or the name of someone you choose to be used for a character in <u>one</u> upcoming novel.

- **Ultimate Reader Level at $49.99 per month...**

All the benefits from the above levels, plus your name or the name of someone you choose (in addition to the one named under the Gold level!) to be used for a <u>major recurring character</u> in upcoming novels.

Visit
www.patreon.com/pastorstephengrantfellowship

If you need to get things done and wish to be inspired, then order Ray Keating's...

The Realistic Optimist TO DO List & Calendar 2019

Available at Amazon.com
Signed editions at www.raykeatingonline.com

Get organized; make things happen; and be inspired throughout the year with *The Realistic Optimist TO DO List & Calendar 2019*. It's a tool that makes sense for career, business, education, faith, family, fun and pretty much everything else in life.

The Realistic Optimist TO DO List & Calendar 2019 offers a simple, systematic combination of long run, weekly and daily TO DO lists that make a real difference in getting things done. For good measure, each page includes a quote from a leader or thinker that in some way reflects being a realistic optimist - providing inspiration, giving pause to think, helping you move ahead, generating a laugh, or eliciting agreement or a roll of the eyes.

Keating concludes, "The fact that you set goals, think about how to achieve those goals, and choose to seek out and use tools like *The Realistic Optimist TO DO List & Calendar* mean that you are a realistic optimist. Forge ahead!"

Visit *DisneyBizJournal.com*

News, Analysis and Reviews of the Disney Entertainment Business!

DisneyBizJournal.com is a media site providing news, information and analysis for anyone who has an interest in the Walt Disney Company, and its assorted ventures, operations, and history. Fans (Disney, Pixar, Marvel, Star Wars, Indiana Jones, and more), investors, entrepreneurs, executives, teachers, professors and students will find valuable information, analysis, and commentary in its pages.

DisneyBizJournal.com is run by Ray Keating, who has experience as a newspaper and online columnist, economist, business teacher and speaker, novelist, movie and book reviewer, podcaster, and more.

Tune in to Ray Keating's Authors and Entrepreneurs Podcast

This entertaining podcast brings together authors, aspiring authors, entrepreneurs, and aspiring entrepreneurs for an exploration of the world of authors as entrepreneurs. Designed with readers and book lovers in mind, the podcast discusses the creative and business aspects of being a writer, and what that means for authors themselves as well as for the reading public. Keating interviews interesting guests, and serves up assorted insights and ideas.

Listen in and subscribe at iTunes, or on Buzzsprout at http://www.buzzsprout.com/147907.

Enjoy
"Chuck" vs. the Business World: Business Tips on TV by Ray Keating

Paperbacks and for the Kindle at Amazon.com

Signed books at raykeatingonline.com

Among Ray Keating's nonfiction books is *"Chuck" vs. the Business World: Business Tips on TV*. In this book, Keating finds career advice, and lessons on managing or owning a business in a fun, fascinating and unexpected place, that is, in the television show *Chuck*.

Keating shows that TV spies and nerds can provide insights and guidelines on managing workers, customer relations, leadership, technology, hiring and firing people, and balancing work and personal life. Larry Kudlow of CNBC says, "Ray Keating has taken the very funny television series *Chuck*, and derived some valuable lessons and insights for your career and business."

If you love *Chuck*, you'll love this book. And even if you never watched *Chuck*, the book lays out clear examples and quick lessons from which you can reap rewards.

59260139R00066

Made in the USA
Middletown, DE
10 August 2019